DEAD

MAN'S

COIN

First Published 2023
Copyright © Saena Tetlow 2023

Published by The Squeeze Press
an Imprint of Wooden Books LTD
Red Brick Building, Glastonbury, BA6 9FT

A CIP catalogue record for this book
is available from the British Library.

ISBN-10: 1-906069-19-0
ISBN-13: 978-1-906069-19-3

Designed and typeset by Wooden Books LTD, UK.
Printed and bound in Great Britain by Clays Ltd, Elcograf S.p.A.

www.woodenbooks.com

the
SQUEEZE
PRESS

THE ADVENTURES OF
ROSIE LIGHTWING

DEAD MAN'S COIN

SAENA TETLOW

PROLOGUE

A SCREAM IN THE NIGHT

VENICE WAS COLD that night.
The kind of cold that seeps in through your clothes and chills you to the bone. The kind of cold that sends you shivering and tightening your coat, as icy talons dig into your skin. The kind of cold that chases you round corners when you aren't looking and attacks you from behind when you least expect it to.

However, the cold would not halt the ever-growing festivities. Large crowds roamed around the streets, wearing masks, extravagant dresses and shirts, top hats and sparkling jewellery.

Gondolas glided on the surface of the dark canal, people sitting inside, talking happily; couples kissing under the starlit sky; mothers, fathers and children, telling made up tales to each other, to distract themselves from the bitter chill that crept up their skin like a long, cold snake, biting into their flesh.

Only a few gondolas remained tied to the bank, bobbing gently on the water, as if in rhythm to the slow, drawling music that came from the streets and courtyards.

But over the happy cheers, drums beating and cheerful exclamations, nobody stopped, or heard the scream.

Someone with a keen ear might have just been able to pick it *out, but to no avail.*

Nobody could have saved the poor soul.

Then, to everyone's surprise, the sky erupted with the low booms of thunder, lightning shattered through the noise, and somewhere in the distance, it started to rain.

I

COIN AND FEATHER

Through the half-open window, a soft breeze drifted in, rustling the pale yellow daffodils that lay in the porcelain vase on the sill. They quivered against the draught and a few petals floated soundlessly on to the floor.

The wind rustled the pages of Rosie's open book, and she looked up. Her room was bare, save for the bed and a short wardrobe that neatly displayed two aged picture frames. The floorboards were scuffed and scratched, creaking under her bare feet, as she moved over to open her dresser. She found it slightly emptier than she had remembered; three thick gowns hung limply on old wooden hangers; two pairs of tatty black heels lay at the bottom, leaving space for a small, withering cardboard box, half-filled with a few of her belongings.

Having hurriedly dressed, Rosie headed downstairs.

She found Agatha already awake, poking the end of her cane into the reduced ashes of a fire.

Agatha looked up, smiled dryly, then returned her gaze to the smouldering pile of ashes.

Agatha was old; face wrinkled, hands trembling, despite the strong grip she had on her cane. Her long hair was always pulled into a tight bun, her expressions were dry and unforgiving. She sat straight, her feet pointed, her back upright, her hands resting on the sides of her chair.

'Stand straighter, darling, your posture is unforgivable.' Agatha's accent was piercing and sharp, and Rosie pulled her shoulders back.

'You're awake early,' Rosie commented. Agatha nodded, rising from her chair with grace.

'I have a morning student,' she said, heading for the door. She pulled a dark green coat over her shoulders and tightened her grip on her cane. Waving an abrupt goodbye, she shut the door and left Rosie to her thoughts. Rosie wished luck upon whoever Agatha was teaching, having left her dance studio many times with tears forming behind her eyes.

A soft squawk was heard from the window, and Rosie looked up. Razario was perched on the sill, facing away from the glass, biting the feathers under his wing.

'Morning, Raz,' Rosie said, stroking the feathers under his beak.

'Good morning,' he replied with a croak, dragging out the letters in a sing-song fashion. Rosie smiled and opened the window, giving him enough room to fly out. He did so, a single feather falling from his tail, floating down to land softly on the windowsill, the bright streak of red catching against the sunlight and looking almost as if it were sparkling.

Rosie hadn't had Razario long; her grandfather had given him to her as a gift, before he had set off on another adventure.

Rosie had begged to go with him every time, and every time, side-stepping the issue, he patted her on the shoulder, telling her that she was too young; or that he would maybe let her when she was older – although Rosie suspected there was another reason for it.

But one soft spring morning, he had woken her up with a sparkle in his blue eyes.

'I have a surprise for you, Rosie,' he'd said. He handed her a map, covered in crosses and strange poems, the words tangling together as if they had been caught in a hurriedly woven spider web. By the end of the hour, Rosie had solved all the clues, answered each riddle with ease, and found the location of the treasure that had been hidden. And that treasure happened to be Razario, nestled in a large silver cage.

'Well done, Rosie,' he'd said, making her jump and chuckle.

She had turned around to thank her grandfather, but found him walking away from her. He moved, and for a moment, his smile faltered. Something seemed to darken behind his eyes, like a fire being put out, but he lifted a hand and waved. There was a difference to his movements; stiff and restricted, and Rosie got the feeling he wouldn't be back for a while.

She'd been right. He had never returned. He'd left her in the care of his old family friend, with nothing more than a couple of paintings, a few coins, and the large grey parrot, who had soon become her only friend.

Snapping back to the present, Rosie grabbed a piece of toast as she headed towards the front door. She threw her coat around her shoulders, put on low heels, a brimmed hat with a thick red ribbon around it, and a pair of dark amber gloves. She locked the heavy wooden door behind her, then turned to face the canal.

Rosie always made a point of noticing something new each morning. Today, the old lady who always brought six oranges from the friendly man on the corner only bought four for some reason, and the three children who usually ran around the street, throwing a ball to one another weren't there.

She'd always hoped that she'd notice something remarkably

distinctive, something she hadn't seen before, though she was never entirely sure what that would be.

Maybe today would be different, she told herself, though she quickly shook the thought from her head. She had the same idea each morning, and each morning, she did exactly the same thing: a short walk, a couple of hours work in the familiar, light blue boat, then back to Agatha's. Whatever changes she noticed had never lived up to her expectations; the amount of people walking by the canal, the number of fruits someone bought at the stall, it was never exciting enough to grab her attention.

And so, day by day, Rosie went over the unchanging routine.

She didn't get paid much for her work, though she didn't need the money; it was only for food, clothes, and the occasional flowers to top up her vase. It was the matter of independence that excited Rosie the most; the walk across the canal, the possibility for adventure, the idea that she could be anywhere at any time, even if her peers disagreed; Rosie was never one for doing what people told her.

She walked slowly, taking in the usual surroundings. To her right, the buildings towered above her, casting long shadows on the cobbled paths. The sun radiated pale crimson highlights on the canal, the water rippled in the breeze. Seagulls circled above the buildings, their croaks and caws drifting over the wind.

On the other side of the canal, the path seemed busier; people shoved their way through bustling crowds, or stopped briefly to buy fruit from the small marquees. Children raced by, dodging past pillars, running across bridges. Gatherings filed in and out of a large building, chatting loudly. Rosie passed a group of women excitedly describing the costumes they were going to wear that evening.

The ribbons of Rosie's hat billowed in the wind, twisting and swirling behind her as she walked on, watching.

Rosie always fantasised about a boat of her own – not a gondola, but a real boat, like grandfather had, one with a deck and a cockpit, and a captain's cabin that she could claim as her own.

Rosie stopped at the boat and looked up.

It was bigger than the others around it, with pale blue paint on the outside, chipping slightly near the edges.

Much to Rosie's displeasure, the boat's name was *Hope,* a rather clichéd and unimaginative title in her opinion, though she'd never spoken her mind, for fear of losing her job. There was a large captain's box at the stern, overlooking the bright canal.

A small staircase led to a ravishing room below deck, featuring a table, chairs, and neat shelves with treasures displayed on them. It was Rosie's favourite place in the boat, and she would spend as long as she could admiring the objects shining under the light, occasionally sketching them in her small pocket notebook.

Rosie stepped on deck and made her way to the door.

She frowned at the sight before her. The ship was in a state far worse than she had remembered it being. The deck was scratched, and there were marks of dried mud scattered around.

She opened the door to find the bannister for the stairs fractured, and the bottom step cracked, splinters splaying in all directions.

The furrows on Rosie's brows deepened. Something wasn't right.

Although she had expected the normally spotless boat to be a little more chaotic than usual, this was something entirely different.

A small gasp escaped Rosie's lips when she saw what was at the bottom of the stairs. Broken pottery shards lay strewn across the floor, scattered aimlessly on its cold wooden surface, the tablecloth was ripped and crumpled, and a bottle of red wine was spilt over its surface, staining the cream cloth. Water leaked from the metal basin on the side of the cabin, overflowing down the edges, spilling droplets onto the floor.

Rosie turned on her heels without thinking, walking back up to the deck. She moved hastily towards the captain's box, putting out her gloved hand to shove it open.

However, as soon as her palm met with the cold painted wood, the door swayed backwards, hitting the wall and swinging towards her again. She frowned and ran her fingers along the side of the wood, careful not to catch any splinters.

The hinges were loose.

Rosie inhaled sharply when the metallic reek hit her nose. She stepped into the room, closing the door behind her. The room was dark on its own, and the glass was slightly duller in shade; she was forced to squint and step closer to get a better look inside.

As she moved forward, her eyes widened and her breath hitched.

There was something no – *someone* – lying on the wooden floor. The sunlight rippled off it, making the shape clearer for Rosie to see. He lay face down on the wood, one arm bent awkwardly under the torso, the other spread out, fingers outstretched, nails bitten to the quick.

Although Rosie couldn't see the body, she knew he was no longer alive. Something seemed to tickle the back of her neck and she snapped her head round to make sure she was alone.

There was no one there. The room was bare, save for an old set of shelves crammed with books, a small wooden chair and a table. The table was covered with a box of shining treasures, similar to the ones downstairs, though they looked slightly shinier and more valuable, and a decanter, half-filled with a shimmering pale golden liquid.

Rosie turned her attention to the body, stepping closer to get a better look. The difference of temperatures hit her face and she gasped. It felt like stepping out of her warm house and onto the windy street. Something told Rosie that the man lying in front of her had died during the early hours of the morning, though she wasn't sure why that was.

It was probably something grandfather had said.

He taught her virtually everything she knew, and if there was any reason for her to know about dead bodies, it would have been he who had given her the information.

She struggled to pull the man's arm from underneath his limp body, tugging at it until it slid free. She was sure that it was broken. She took off her gloves and placed her hand on the man's arm. She was hesitant, as if he was in disapproval of her actions. His skin was stone cold. She shivered.

Rosie pulled the man's sleeve back, noting in her mind the fabric – a rough, drab cut, poorly stitched.

Hesitating, possibly for the first time since she saw the body, Rosie turned it round to get a better look at its face, taking in important details – throat tight, lips chafed and rather blue, eyes unblinking, glassy, looking into nothing, but at the same time, staring directly at her, deep into her soul. His cheeks were cold, like wet stone, and on the side of his head, a deep cut slashed into his skin.

Rosie grimaced. That must have been how he died.

'What am I doing?' she whispered to herself. Her voice seemed to linger in the empty room, as if the walls were listening to her.

Surely she shouldn't be alone with a corpse – she should go and get the authorities right now.

'No,' she said aloud, almost as if she were talking to the man lying in front of her. Her eyes were fixed on his unmoving stare, and she felt a sudden stab of sympathy for him. He looked so young. Surely he didn't deserve this? What about his family? If he had any. They should know what happened to him.

Taking a slow breath inwards, Rosie nodded to herself. She wouldn't leave. She would stay, and discover this poor man's killer. She wasn't sure why, but she knew it was possible. She could do it. She could solve this crime.

She needed evidence, she told herself, digging her gloved hand into his left pocket and pulling out a keychain, with three keys attached to it, a crumpled piece of paper and a penknife. She turned her attention to the keychain. It was copper, the metal bluing where water had touched it. On it hung three keys, one long and thin with the number '3' engraved on the top. The shortest one was made of brass, and had three, uneven teeth. But it was the last key that caught Rosie's eye.

It was the shortest of the three, with intricate curves and spirals on the bow. But it was covered from top to bottom in a green substance, which had dried and crusted.

Rosie sniffed it. It smelled old and damp, like an abandoned alleyway, and it made her head hurt.

Reaching into her pocket, Rosie pulled out a dark red notebook and a pencil, writing down notes, including a sketch of the keys, which she put back where she had found them. Rosie then turned to the piece of paper, unfolding it, making sure not to tear it in the process. On it, carefully scrawled across the paper in black ink, there was a name of a house, along with the number '3'.

Rosie noted this down, hoping that it somehow related to

the number etched into the key.

Picking up the penknife, Rosie opened each blade to make sure there were no traces of blood on them. There weren't any, so she put the knife and paper back in the man's pocket.

Rosie put her hand in the right pocket of the man's trousers, ignoring the shiver that ran down her spine. It was empty. Turning back to her notebook, Rosie made sure she had written down everything she needed, then turned to leave.

As she stood, however, her hand brushed against something stiff in the sleeve of his shirt. Rosie frowned. It didn't have any pockets, and there was no place to hide anything inside it.

Crouching down, Rosie turned over the cuff of his sleeve. Her eyes widened.

Sewn into the fabric was a small hexagonal coin. It was fastened to the material with tight stitches, the face of it pressed against the cloth.

Rosie tugged at it with prying fingers, and the stitches came loose.

The coin fell from the man's shirt and tumbled to the floor. It rolled on its side and began to spin, letting off a strange trembling rattle, until it decided to give up and lie flat on the wood with a dull clatter. Rosie knelt to pick it up, but dropped it almost immediately, as if it had burned her.

She had seen this coin before.

She was seven. She was in her grandfather's study, looking through his desk. She knew she shouldn't be there, but she couldn't help herself.

Her grandfather always had such interesting things in his study. Her eyes travelled to a shell on the desk, twice the size of her hand, covered in something that sparkled in the sunlight. She held it up to her ear and closed her eyes. She could almost hear the ocean, the crashing of angry waves, and swirling of water, the dragging of tides against the sand. Putting down the shell, Rosie opened the desk drawer and pulled out a coin. It was hexagonal, with a crescent moon circling a small hole, and washed out markings of feathers running along its edge.

Rosie felt as if it were heating the palm of her hand.

She would have continued staring at it, if her grandfather hadn't walked into the study.

Caught off guard, Rosie dropped the coin onto the table. For a split second, something almost like sadness flitted across her grandfather's face. Then it vanished, as quick as mist evaporating into the sky.

He smiled. 'You shouldn't be in here, Rosie. You know that.'

'Sorry.' Rosie dropped her gaze. 'I— I didn't mean to.'

Her grandfather smiled again. 'It's okay. Run along now, Rosie. I have something important to do.'

Rosie hurried out of the room.

Years later, she had mustered up the courage to ask him where the coin came from. He looked up at her with a curious gaze. 'There actually aren't any left,' he said in a raspy voice. 'This is the last one you'll ever see, trust me.' Then he returned to his book, head bent low over the weathered pages.

Snapping back to the present, Rosie stared at the coin on the floor, hardly able to believe it. She bent down and picked it up, twirling it between her fingers.

After a moment's consideration, she dropped the coin into her coat pocket, feeling as though it was weighing down her clothes.

Rosie walked over to the door and turned the handle.

As soon as it opened, she stumbled back. There were two men standing outside, clad in black uniforms and flat caps, with shining handcuffs tied to their belts.

II

TARNISHED SILVER

ROSIE GASPED and stepped backwards, tripping a little. The policemen looked at her, their eyes moving to the body in the middle of the room, then back to her again.

'I didn't do it, I swear,' Rosie said, cursing herself for sounding so unsure.

'I'd like you to put your arms in the air, *signorina*.' The taller policeman reached into his coat and drew out a pair of handcuffs. Rosie slowly drew her hands out of her pockets, holding them over her head, taking a quick breath inwards to stop them from trembling.

The policeman walked forward, pulled Rosie's hands in front of her and secured them together with the cuffs. They were old and tarnished, and Rosie got the impression they hadn't been used many times.

Her heart was in her throat, her chest rising and falling shakily.

'I found the body here ... he was already dead,' she tried to explain, as the second man walked over to the body on the floor and placed two fingers on his neck.

'Why were you on this boat?' The taller man demanded.

'I work here,' Rosie was determined to keep her voice from shaking.

'What sort of work?' The man asked her calmly.

'I clean.' Rosie's tone was bitter, as she thought this a rather obvious question to ask a young lady.

'And when did you find the body?' Clearly, the policeman was not convinced. His bark brown eyes were narrowed, his large hands rough against Rosie's, gripping them tightly so that didn't she didn't try to escape.

'About half an hour ago.'

'And is there a reason why you didn't tell the authorities right away?'

'I don't know ... I couldn't.'

'You felt guilty?' If possible, his eyes narrowed even more. He turned to look at the body on the floor, and something in the way his jaw tightened told Rosie that he didn't have much experience. He seemed to be wary, as if he believed the body would get up and walk out at any given moment.

'No, I told you I didn't do it!' She knew they were trying to get her to confess, and she wouldn't fall for it. The man next to the body looked up.

'He's dead.'

Rosie rolled her eyes. 'Of course he's dead, he's been dead for hours!'

As soon as the words tumbled out of her mouth, Rosie knew she'd made a mistake. Both men eyed her suspiciously, looking at one another, then back to her again.

'Let's go back to the station, *signorina*. You can answer my questions there.'

'But I didn't kill him!'

The man holding Rosie shook his head and spoke clearly.

'You can say that all back in the office.'

He nodded at the man kneeling by the body, then opened the door and walked through, pulling a reluctant Rosie behind him.

ROSIE AND THE POLICEMAN walked to the station in silence, passing a small number of people shopping in the market, some buying outfits for the second night of the Carnival, others simply getting essentials for their day. There were visitors walking up and down the same street, not wanting to admit that they were lost, and children running to school, their mothers calling for them to be careful near the water.

A few people stopped to stare at the officer walking briskly, a fifteen-year-old girl in tow, not looking particularly celebratory about her current situation. The officer turned left and walked up the steps of an old building, just off the side of the canal.

It was a large, square construction, the stone chipping off the sides, leaving small holes in the brickwork. The windows at the top of the building were dirty, and birds perched on the low hanging edge of the flat roof, calling out to each other loudly. Hanging over the door was a large black sign that read: *Polizia*.

The officer ushered Rosie into the building and followed her inside. The low ceiling was decorated in tiled pictures of stars and geometric patterns. There were a few desks in the room, where busy workers were writing quickly on yellowed pieces of paper, or sitting opposite someone, nodding whilst documenting things in scribbly handwriting.

A young man was using the telephone in the corner, muttering quickly and nodding to a boy standing next to him, who wrote something down in a small notebook.

The policeman guided Rosie into a small room, closing

the wooden door behind him. He pointed to a padded chair and Rosie sat down, placing her cuffed hands in her lap, gripping them so tightly her knuckles were turning white. The policeman sat in a chair opposite her, interlocking his huge fingers and setting them on the table in front of him.

'My name is Enzo. I just need you to answer a few questions, *signorina* ... ' He trailed off and looked over at her expectantly.

'Rosie,' she muttered, 'Rosie Lightwing.' She gave him what she hoped was an innocent smile.

'...Lightwing,' he sounded as if he didn't believe she'd even given him the correct name. '... you found the body, is that right?'

'Yes,' said Rosie quietly.

'And what time was this?'

'Nine o'clock, I think.' Rosie remembered hearing the clock tower bells chiming loudly through the muffled window of the boat.

'And we found you at nine thirty ... So what were you doing all that time?'

'I—' For a moment, Rosie considered lying. He wouldn't believe her if she told him she was about to investigate. In his eyes, she was only a little girl telling lies to get out of trouble.

'I was looking.' She said at last.

'Looking for what, *signorina*?'

'For ... clues'

'Clues?' Clearly, Enzo was not convinced.

'Yes. For ideas about who killed him.'

'Are you telling me, *Signorina*... that you, a *child*, were trying to investigate a murder?' He was incredulous, his brow furrowing into a rollercoaster-ride of confusion and amusement.

'Yes ... that's precisely what I was doing.'

Enzo laughed hollowly. 'You expect me to believe you?'

'That's what I was hoping for.' Regaining her composure, Rosie spoke coolly, as if they were just having a normal conversation, and she was not a suspect in a murder investigation, which only angered Enzo further, causing him to lean forward in his chair.

'Listen,' Rosie started, keeping her tone level. 'There's no way I could've killed him.'

Enzo lifted an eyebrow. 'And ... why's that?' He asked, his voice thick with amusement.

'I'm a child! A fifteen-year-old girl! It's practically impossible for someone like me to kill a man over double my size and strength.'

Enzo nodded, but his smirk didn't fade. 'Actually it is possible,' he said. 'You could've snuck up on him, or hit him from a higher angle.'

Rosie rolled her eyes. 'Why would I even want to kill him? And why would I be in a boat, alone with a stranger?'

Enzo's smirk faltered, but his reply was drowned out by a knock on the door. The officer from the boat entered the room and walked over to Enzo, whispering something into his ear, before leaving hastily.

Rosie blinked, as if waiting for Enzo to repeat what he had just heard.

'I have just been informed by my colleague of the time of death,' he started, pausing for a moment, almost for dramatic effect. 'My question for you ... Miss Lightwing ... is what you were doing between midnight and two last night?'

'I was sleeping.' Rosie hoped this was believable enough, because although she could have made up a lie about being at the Carnival, if she was proven wrong, things would be even more complicated.

'Right. That's all I need to know.' He stood up and Rosie breathed a small sigh of relief. Then he spoke again, and his voice was cold.

'Rosie Lightwing, you are under arrest for murder. Stand up, please.'

'What? No! Wait!' Rosie struggled against Enzo's grip, as he held her tightly, shoving her out of the room. He only made it about three steps, however, when an angry shout filled the air, followed by a crack of wood hitting the stone.

'*CHE STAI FACENDO?!*'

The voice echoed through the office and Rosie turned. A woman stood in the entrance of the building, shaking with anger. She stood tall and straight, despite her evidently old age. Her hair was pulled up in a tight bun, exposing her creased and not particularly friendly face. In her right hand she held a long, wooden cane, polished and gleaming off the light in the room. Rosie's heart leapt.

'Agatha!'

Agatha marched over to where Rosie and Enzo were standing and put her face inches away from Enzo's. Taken by surprise, he stepped back a little.

'*Come ti permetti?!*' Agatha shouted, and everyone in the room seemed to hold their breaths.

'Arresting this innocent child with no evidence! You should be ashamed of yourselves!'

Enzo cowered slightly. 'I— we— we saw her at the scene of the crime!'

'She works there, fool!' Agatha yelled at the top of her voice, 'uncuff her NOW!'

Rosie smiled, because she noticed that although Enzo's hands were hardly trembling, they were trembling, nonetheless. He drew out a key from his pocket and shakily unlocked Rosie's cuffs. They fell to the floor, clanging when they hit the stone, and Rosie rubbed her wrists. She made a mental note to buy Agatha fresh flowers, as a token of her appreciation, although she'd probably turn them down with a scoff.

'Now then!' Agatha jabbed the end of her cane into Enzo's chest, pushing him backward even more.

'When your investigation comes to a dead end, don't come chasing after Rosie to put in prison! She was in my house all night, so she had nothing to do with the crime ... *Capisci?*' she added, clicking her fingers in front of his face with an angry sigh.

'*Sì, signora*' he said, voice cracking.

'Good. Rosie, come with me.' Agatha beckoned Rosie to follow her.

'Oh, and you,' she muttered, turning around again to point at Enzo.

'*Sì, signora?*' he asked, his voice a quiet murmur.

'You should take that awful hat off. It really shadows your eyes.'

'*Sì, signora.*' He slowly took the hat off and placed it in his hands, revealing his short, dark hair.

'Much better.' Agatha patted his cheek with her wrinkled hand.

Then, without saying another word, she pulled Rosie out of the building, slamming the door with such force that the windows rattled on their hinges.

III

A DIFFICULT DECISION

As soon as the door closed, Agatha turned to Rosie with daggers behind her eyes.

'What *were* you thinking? Staying in the room with a dead body? What did you expect would happen?'

'I—I don't know. I'm sorry,' Rosie stammered, backing away, breathing heavily.

'Just ... don't go doing that again, will you? I don't fancy having to bail you out of prison every time you go to work.'

Rosie smiled. 'Thank you,' she said.

Agatha didn't answer, and instead took off her shoes and stepped into the living room. Rosie pulled off her coat, hung it on the rusted hook, and followed her in.

Inside, two cushioned armchairs sat opposite a fireplace, half full with logs. A thick rug lined the floor, covering the ageing floorboards, and in a far corner, a grandfather clock announced the time. The room smelt of baked bread and smoke – rich and welcoming, and Rosie inhaled it with a smile.

In the kitchen, two short chairs sat either side of a table, which was covered in a lacy cloth. A large gilded frame hung above the sink, showing a broad green field, dotted with pink and yellow flowers, a white mountain looming in the background.

Agatha made tea, placed the nearest cup to Rosie and took a seat. Rosie couldn't help but feel as if she were in trouble as she sat down and took the cup in her hands.

'Rosie,' Agatha started, her fingers gripping the edge of the table. 'Are you going to investigate this murder or not?'

'I—'

'Because you should.' Her face was earnest.

Rosie shifted her focus from to the table, looking up into Agatha's cold grey eyes.

'Why?' she fixed Agatha with a hard stare.

Agatha paused, as if debating whether or not to speak. 'Aren't you curious? You just found a body. Don't you want to know what happened?'

'Why do *I* need to solve it?' Rosie demanded in a whisper. 'I'm fifteen!'

Once again, Agatha paused. She cleared her throat and leant back in her chair, resting her hands against her cane.

'What would Alfred think?' she questioned.

'What?' Rosie stared at her, 'What does my grandfather have to do with any of this?'

'Rosie, listen.' Agatha spoke in a hushed voice, as if scared someone might be listening.

'I can't explain it all, but trust me when I tell you, you'll find answers. Perhaps investigating this would be good, a change.'

'A change?'

Going for a walk, or cutting your hair was something you did as a change, not investigate a murder that would likely put you in serious danger.

Agatha fell silent, and Rosie stared at her aimlessly. She

leaned back in her chair and rubbed her hands over her knees. She was surprised she'd even *thought* of investigating. Surely, she shouldn't. She was only a child, and murder was not something to play around with.

She thought of how easily she'd looked at the lifeless body back on the boat. Anyone else would have gone straight to the police; so ... why hadn't she? What had made her stay and look for clues? It wasn't just that she was bored; surely her cure to boredom wouldn't be to solve a murder.

Maybe it was the feeling, she thought.

The rush of adrenaline, the prickling sense on the back of her neck, the way her eyes had widened.

She thought back to the body in the boat. The sad, glassy eyes, the broken arm, the wound on the back of his head.

Rosie thought of the coin. The way it glinted in her hand, the burning feeling that had spread across her palm when she had touched it, the words her grandfather had told her; *that there weren't any left.*

Her mind was made up.

'Very well,' she said. 'I'll do it.'

Agatha smiled, giving her an approving nod.

Rosie placed her cup on the table and folded her hands. 'Where should I begin?'

IV

SPIRALLING LIES

AGATHA CLOSED HER EYES.
'You should start with suspects.' She stood up and began to pull a loaf of bread from the cupboard, along with a plate of various cheeses.

'I suggest talking to *Signore* Romano.' She spoke with a bitterness in her voice, as if she was biting on ice. A few months ago, he had referred to her as an *"old woman"* after she had corrected his stance. She had borne a grudge against him ever since, and often scolded Rosie for continuing to work for him.

Rosie pulled her notebook from her coat pocket, flipping to the page that was needed.

Agatha smiled. 'I'm impressed. You know what you're doing.'

Rosie nodded. She contemplated telling Agatha about the coin, which was the main reason she had even *considered* investigating, but decided against it, for reasons she was not yet sure of. She knew Agatha would not approve of her chasing after clues on an inanimate object that apparently didn't even exist anymore.

'I should go out then,' she said instead, cramming food into her mouth as she stood up and headed for the door.

Agatha looked at her. She opened her mouth, and for a moment, something flashed across her face. Rosie couldn't quite make it out.

Worry? Excitement? Pity?

But then it was gone, and she nodded, closing her mouth.

'Good luck, Rosie,' she said.

'Thanks.' Rosie placed her hand on the doorknob. As she put on her coat, she paused and looked back at Agatha sitting at the table. She was hiding something, Rosie knew it. She was hiding something important.

IT WAS A COLD DAY; dark clouds gathered over the sun, blocking away the light. The wind blew harshly, forcing young ladies to hold tightly to the brims of their hats and hurry along the narrow cobbles.

Rosie walked with confidence, her hands tight fists in their leather gloves, the bottom of her dress swinging breezily with each step she took. Her short black hair kept falling in front of her face, forcing her to brush the stray strands away from her eyes every few steps.

It was not a long walk to the boat, but Rosie took her time, thinking about what she was getting herself into.

There were so many reasons for her to turn around, retreat to Agatha's house and forget this had ever happened. She could go back to how things were merely hours before, back to her simple life of cleaning ships and roaming around the cramped alleyways. But Rosie did not turn around; instead, she walked faster.

She crossed a short bridge, bumping into people standing by the edge, looking out at the canal.

The loud buzz of chattering voices and soft lapping of

water against buildings filled her ears as she walked. The streets smelled old and musty, a strange mixture of sea water and mould, a scent she was used to by now.

She crossed another bridge, keeping her eyes fixed on the canal beside her. The water rippled and shone under the partial sun, small sparkles shimmering off its surface. Rosie stepped off the bridge, arriving at the *Hope*. The words were now just a tangled mess of spiralling lies, curling up the side of the light blue boat. It was a sight she once loved, although as she glanced at it, it did not seem so inviting.

As Rosie neared the boat, she stopped, noticing two policemen and *Signore* Romano talking by the edge of the steps. They were facing the boat, and neither of them saw Rosie walk past and hide behind a barrel, peeking out so that she was still within earshot.

Rosie leaned closer, noticing Enzo speaking with *Signore* Romano. She watched as Romano moved his hands in ridiculous gestures as he spoke, while Enzo nodded and turned to his notebook, scribbling quickly as he tried to keep up with Romano's story.

As much as Rosie wanted to step closer, she knew she couldn't show her face to the police, especially after her close brush with disaster, so she kept her distance.

'I see,' Enzo was saying. 'And where were you last night between midnight and two in the morning?'

'I was at the Carnival, like most people,' Romano said. He had an edge to his voice, and a smile that was too forced – one that disappeared the moment Enzo turned back to his book.

'Right. And you don't know why this man was in your boat?'

'No, I don't. I've never actually met the poor fellow!'

Enzo looked up. 'You don't know who he is?'

'Oh, everyone knows who he is! His name was Nico

Lomobardi, an explorer. He'd just come back from South America, you know?'

'Right,' Enzo said, with hardly any interest in his voice. 'And do you know what ship they went on?'

'How could I *not* know? The ship's name was *Liberty*. It's still docked at the port, if I remember correctly.'

Signore Romano said the name with such praise in his voice, he could have been talking about Gods, and Rosie sighed; *another clichéd name*, she thought to herself.

Enzo nodded in acknowledgment and quickly scribbled something down.

'Excellent. Just a couple more questions and I'll be out of your hair.'

Rosie wanted to listen longer, but, thinking it a good time to leave, she turned away, keeping her head low.

ON HER WAY TO THE PORT, Rosie stopped to buy an iced bun from a small shop on the corner of the canal. As she was paying, she noticed with a sigh how much lighter her purse was getting. Perhaps her work at the boat *wasn't* paying enough.

At the port, she paused to take in the view. The air was thick with the smell of salt and seaweed, a clear difference to the murky, old scent of the canals.

The paths were busy, with people bustling this way and that, workers hauling crates onto large ships ready to set sail, travellers gaping at the magnificent sight of the sea. It never ceased to amaze her: the way the seagulls flitted above the water, diving at the first sight of food, the way the waves lapped hungrily at the stone before slowly sliding back onto itself, the way the sea caught the rays of sun causing sparkles to litter its surface.

She loved the way the boats lined up next to each other, the different curves and sails clashing beautifully. After a few minutes of looking, Rosie finally found the *Liberty*. It was huge, with three tall wooden masts, reaching into the sky, white sails tied tightly to the wood, so as not to blow away in the wind. There was a figurehead at the bowsprit, a lady with long plaits tied behind her head, her eyes closed, her mouth curved into an elegant smile.

The outer hull of the boat was painted black, with the word *Liberty* curling up the side of it in thin, spider web lines of shimmering gold.

Rosie stepped onto the wooden deck and headed straight over to the captain's cabin, her boots tapping on the polished floor.

When she reached the cabin, Rosie hesitated. She had not thought about what she would say once she got there.

Excuse me? I'm a fifteen-year-old girl investigating a murder because my ancient dance teacher told me to. Do you think you could answer some questions about a dead explorer who worked with you?

She smirked. *That would work*, she thought sarcastically.

'May I help you?' someone asked from behind her.

Rosie turned to see a tall man with long, dark brown hair tied back into a ponytail. He was wearing a large blue velvet coat done up with bright gold buttons that shimmered against the sun. His shoes were almost as shiny as the deck, reflecting off every inch of light.

'*Buongiorno*,' Rosie said. 'I'm looking to speak to the captain of this ship.'

'That would be me.' He replied, 'I'm Liam.' He spoke with a thick Irish accent, his voice rich and smooth, like melted butter.

He smiled at her, and Rosie paused.

'I was wondering if you could answer a few questions about

someone who worked with you?'

Liam smiled. 'Of course,' he said, and ushered her into his cabin.

Inside the room, he gestured for Rosie to sit on a chair opposite a wooden table, laden with miniature treasures; crystals glittered and sparkled, catching the light and reflecting rainbows off every corner of the room.

A small skull stood behind a globe of the world, which was spinning slowly on its axis. There was a map on the table, with a compass lying on it. A sextant was perched neatly next to a bowl of fresh fruit, its intricate complexity calling out for Rosie to reach over and touch it, and she had to hold her fingers tightly together to compose herself.

Liam sat down opposite her and crossed his legs.

'And what do you wish to know?'

'Someone was working here,' Rosie started. 'His name was Nico. I was wondering if you could tell me what you know about him'

'Has something happened to him?' Liam asked in a worried tone, his brows furrowing.

Rosie paused. 'Yes,' she said at last, 'I'm afraid he's dead.'

'What?! When?' Liam's eyes flashed with a look of horror, and for a fleeting moment, Rosie thought he was going to leap from his chair and throw something across the room. She stayed still and kept her gaze fastened to his face. Although she found herself instinctively gripping her fingers tighter..

'I'm sorry,' Rosie said, adjusting her position, so she was now leaning forward in her chair.

'How do you know he's dead?' Liam's voice was different now – dangerously quiet and icy.

'I found him.' Rosie said, keeping her tone level.

'Where?' Liam demanded sharply.

Rosie hesitated. She could almost feel the anger radiating off him, like the heat from the flames of a raging fire.

'On the *Hope*,' she said. 'It's a boat I work on.'

Liam looked at her, the warmth melted from his eyes.

The calm, inviting look was gone, replaced with a distant, angry expression.

'You say you work there?' he asked.

'Yes ... but I swear to you, I had nothing to do with his death.'

'Right.' He paused, took a slow breath, and seemed to regain his calm composure, sitting back in his chair, folding his hands in his lap.

'And there's something you want to ask me.'

'I need to know more about Nico, if you could tell me.'

'Are you investigating?' he asked, his tone thick with amusement.

Rosie paused. 'Yes.'

Liam had the faint ghost of a smile on his lips. 'What is it you wish to know?'

Rosie thought. She had too many questions, and she knew Liam had neither time nor patience for all of them.

'Anything you can tell me.'

The captain smiled and walked over to a desk. He picked up a bottle filled with dark red liquid and poured himself a glass, then sat back down again, crossing one leg over the other.

'Ask me a question,' he said.

Rosie smiled. *This might be easier than I'd imagined*, she thought.

'You could start by telling me more about him,' she suggested, pulling out her notebook and a short pencil. There were bite marks on the end, and she felt a small rush of embarrassment.

'He's been working with us for twelve years as a navigator. He was planning to see his brother while we stopped off here.'

'Did they get on well?'

Liam nodded. 'They weren't having any issues as far as I was aware,' he muttered.

Rosie acknowledged his words as she scribbled down notes. 'Did Nico have any friends here?' she asked. It was strange how easily the questions came to her. It was as if she'd done this many times before.

Liam nodded. 'Oh yes. Everyone loved him ...,' he trailed off, dropping his gaze to the floor.

'But?' Rosie asked, leaning forward slightly.

'There was someone ...' Liam began. 'He and Nico were always bickering – but not in an aggressive way!' he added quickly. It didn't take Rosie long to understand why. One of his own getting killed was bad enough, but if word got out that there was a murderer on his ship, the rest of the crew would soon lose trust in each other, and a rift would form between them.

'Right,' Rosie bent down, scribbling quickly in her notebook, her small, neatly packed handwriting covering the cream coloured paper. As she wrote, Rosie wished she hadn't been so impatient when trying to learn shorthand from her grandmother.

'Could you tell me the man's name?' she asked. There was a pause, in which Liam diverted his gaze to the floor.

'His name was Gwydion Fosscome,' he said at last. 'He has a house here opposite San Giacomo.'

Rosie nodded, turning her head to her notebook. After writing a short sentence, she looked up again. Although Gwydion was a suspect, she needed something more than a single thread to go on. It was unlikely for her to find the murderer after one visit.

'Listen,' Liam leaned forward in his chair. 'I was with Gwydion for almost all of last night. It's unlikely for him to have killed anyone.'

Rosie paused. 'Do you know of anyone else who might want to hurt Nico?' she asked. Liam shook his head.

'He was on such good terms with everyone he knew, I couldn't imagine anyone wanting to hurt him.'

'Where does Nico's brother live?' Rosie asked after a moment. Liam shrugged. 'I'm not sure. Gwydion may know. He and Nico were friends before their rivalry started. He may have told him.'

Rosie nodded. 'I see,' she said, putting on a small smile. 'Is there anything else you think I should know?' Rosie asked. After a long pause, Liam nodded.

'This is very dangerous business, you know! You're only a child, you don't need to be investigating a murder!'

Rosie looked up from her book in surprise. She had expected him to give her a different reason not to investigate, and she couldn't stop the small smile that creeped onto her face.

'I understand,' she said, 'and I appreciate your concern, but I'm quite determined to see where this leads me.'

'I thought you'd say that,' Liam stood up and walked to the door, gesturing for Rosie to follow.

'Thank you for your time,' she said, reaching out a hand for him to shake. He took it and looked worriedly into her eyes.

'Just promise me one thing.' He bent to her height, his face etched with concern.

'Yes?' Although she knew what to expect, there was still a hint of excitement in her voice.

'Promise me you'll be careful. While I appreciate your

confidence, there are plenty of others who wouldn't approve, and a young lady like yourself should watch out around those types of people.'

He said it with emphasis on the *young lady*, and Rosie knew that was the moral of his sentence. She nodded.

'What about you?' She found herself asking, 'do you mind?'

'No,' he said, without a moment's hesitation, his lips tilting upwards. 'We're all equal under the eyes of God.'

Again, Rosie nodded, her smile broadening.

'But please,' he added, 'be careful.'

'I will.'

Rosie shook his hand, then turned and headed for the Grand Canal.

V

IVORY SMILES

GWYDION'S HOUSE was so tall and thin, that it looked as if it had been squashed together while being built. Stone curves stood above a neatly painted door with a brass handle, and painted vines spiralled and twisted all the way up the sides of the house to the flat roof.

Rosie knocked, and the sound of her three, neat raps echoed through the house. The door opened a few moments later and a young lady peered out through the small gap. She was out of breath, and Rosie noticed a maid retreat behind a wall with a soft scowl.

The girl looked about Rosie's age, but taller, long, honey-coloured hair trailing to her waist like a waterfall.

'Can I help you, miss?' She spoke in a clear British accent, with a voice of forced politeness. She smiled at her, the same way one would if they had been practising the action many times before. She appeared as if she had been carved from bone; perfectly poised posture, unrealistically symmetrical features.

She looked the definition of graceful.

'I hope so. My name's Rosie. I was hoping to talk to Gwydion.'

'May I ask what business you have with him?' The girl's eyes narrowed curiously, but before Rosie could form a reply, a voice cut her off.

'Is there a problem, Kyra?' someone asked, as he stood behind her and placed a hand heavily on her shoulder. 'There's someone here to talk to you.'

The man was barely taller than the young girl beside him, though Rosie could tell he was a good deal older. His hair was blond, like Kyra's, though a little scruffier and darker in shade. It took Rosie just over a second to realise that they were siblings.

'Is there a problem, Miss?' he asked politely, in the same well-spoken tone as Kyra, flashing an identical, pre-rehearsed, ivory smile in Rosie's direction.

'I need to talk to you about Nico Lombardi.'

For a brief moment, surprise flitted across Gwydion's face, then it was gone, and he smiled pleasantly.

'Of course. Please come in.'

He stepped aside, and Rosie walked in, following him through a hall that eventually led to a large room. The walls were painted white, and picture frames hung neatly on their surface. There was a wide portrait of an old man holding a cane, gazing out with defiant eyes, and a smaller one of a woman dressed all in blue, her hair twisted into a curling pile on her head. A large chandelier hung from the ceiling, each tiny crystal teardrop reflecting the light, sending bright flashes across the room. A fire was lit in the corner, letting out the sound of crackling flames and soft snaps of wood.

Kyra disappeared into a small hallway, and Gwydion perched himself on the edge of a sofa, gesturing for Rosie to do the same. She sat, her back straight and her feet planted firmly on the ground, placing her hands in her lap.

'What's wrong with Nico?' he asked, creasing his brow, a

slight smirk on his face, like a child, waiting for his sibling to get in trouble.

'He's dead.' Rosie found it strange how easy it was for her to say that. She looked at Gwydion, studying his expressions. The smirk disappeared as quickly as it had arrived, replaced by a deep frown.

'What? ...' he trailed off and looked down. 'When?'

'Yesterday.' Rosie was taken aback, expecting a smile, a wry comment or a small chuckle, not for him to look like he was about to burst into tears.

'I thought you didn't like him,' Rosie questioned, choosing her words carefully.

'Oh,' he nodded in understanding, 'because we argued a lot? That wasn't hate.'

'What was it then?'

Gwydion paused. 'I'll admit, Nico and I didn't have the greatest relationship. But I would never do something so absurd as to *kill* him! I ... was only jealous of him, really.'

'Why's that? What did he have that you didn't?' Rosie found it hard to believe that someone in a position like Gwydion's could be jealous of anything.

Gwydion hesitated. 'He was Liam's first choice for everything, everyone wanted to be him. I was just angry at him for getting everything *I* wanted.'

Rosie nodded. Although jealousy was a clear motive for murder, she believed him; their rivalry was likely nothing more than childish bickering.

'Then could you tell me where you were last night?' she asked.

'I was at the Carnival with Liam.'

'Did you see Nico?'

'No. I last saw him a couple of days ago. He seemed a little different, but I thought nothing of it.' Gwydion stroked the almost-stubble on his chin, thinking.

'Different how?' Rosie gently tapped her pencil on the ridge of her notebook page.

'He seemed on edge. When I asked him what was wrong, he told me he was having trouble with his family.'

Rosie remembered Liam mentioning Nico's brother.

'Do you know where his brother lives?' She asked.

'About four houses down from here. It's the smallest in the row.' He scoffed a little at that.

'If you thought *our* house looked small, just wait until you see his. At least we have some *class*.' He gave a soft chuckle and shook his head, although he soon stopped once he noticed Rosie wasn't laughing. He cleared his throat and looked away.

'Did he and Nico get on?' Rosie asked.

Gwydion shrugged, 'I'm not sure,' he said. He sighed and looked down, twiddling with his fingers. The room fell quiet, and the soft ticking of the grandfather clock pierced the waiting silence.

After a moment, Gwydion cleared his throat.

'You should tell Alfie.' He looked scared, like a deer caught in its tracks.

Rosie nodded and turned to her notebook, writing in neat, closely packed words.

Do you know if anybody wanted to hurt Nico?' she asked, after she finished writing.

'Actually ...' Gwydion trailed off, his gaze dropping to the floor. Something in his eyes seemed to change and he looked up again. He frowned and shook his head.

'I really don't know why I'm telling you all of this,' he said, as if he only just realised who he was talking to. 'You're a child, and— and I could be leading you into something dangerous.'

Gwydion stood up and began pacing around the room, biting the end of his index finger.

'I think you should go,' he said at last, his tone dry. 'There's nothing else I can tell you.'

Rosie sighed. 'Why the sudden change of heart?' she asked, not moving from her seat. 'You seemed perfectly fine a few minutes ago.'

Once again Gwydion hesitated. 'Look,' he said, taking a seat and leaning forward, placing his elbows on his knees. 'There *is* somebody who had a problem with Nico, but from what I've heard, he's a dangerous man. I don't want to be the cause of you getting into situations in which you can't handle the outcome.'

'I'm aware of the risks,' Rosie said, keeping her voice clear.

'He calls himself *Il Signore di Venezia*. Others know him as The Puzzle Box Maker,' Gwydion breathed, 'but ... nobody knows his real name. It's rumoured he's behind every crime that happens in Venice. I think Nico owed him.'

Rosie thought it was a little presumptuous of someone to name themselves the 'Lord of Venice.'

She closed her notebook and stood up. Her eyes drifted across the room, unsure of where to look. Eventually, she settled for staring at the large white elephant on the mantelpiece.

'Why *are* you investigating?' Gwydion asked quietly from his seat.

'I found the body,' Rosie said. 'I couldn't leave without answers.'

'Right.' Gwydion looked down. 'But ... you're a ...'

'A *girl*?' There was a clear note of annoyance in Rosie's voice. 'I'm aware of that,' she said, looking him in the eyes.

He tore his gaze away, his cheeks turning a deep shade of red.

'I ... I was going to say child but ...' Gwydion trailed off, avoiding her eyes.

'I'm aware of that also.' Rosie smiled pleasantly.

Gwydion opened his mouth, then closed it again with a sigh, dropping his gaze further. Although he fell quiet, Rosie knew what he was going to say.

'Right,' he said at last. 'I wish you the best in your investigation.'

'Thank you,' Rosie answered, with perhaps a little more distaste than she had meant to. She made to leave but was interrupted by a quiet voice from behind her, barely louder than a whisper.

'Excuse me, miss?'

Rosie turned and saw Kyra standing behind her inside the doorway, her hand resting on the doorframe. Rosie could tell she had been listening to the conversation that had just been having; her eyes were slightly wider than was necessary, and her face creased with concern.

'I want to tell you something.'

She nodded, and Kyra gestured with her hand for Rosie to follow her.

They walked through a hallway so thin, Rosie felt as if the walls were closing in on her. The staircase was narrow and the steps short, yet somehow, the building did not look any less glamorous.

Floral wallpaper lined the room Rosie was led into. A large sofa laden with pillows sat in the corner, a mirror hung above a small basin, and a table was scattered with pieces of paper, pencils and charcoal, a high chair beside it, stacked with sheets of brown paper.

Kyra followed Rosie's gaze and walked over to the table. She picked up a piece of paper and showed it to Rosie, whose eyes widened when she saw it. There was a drawing of a girl's face on the page. It was shaded with the skill of a trained artist, the eyes shining, the mouth a contented smile, the hair in a long, flowing plait, a few perfect strands escaping from it, blowing in front of the girl's face.

'It's wonderful,' Rosie muttered.

Kyra smiled and placed the picture back on the messy table and sat on the floor, careful not to tear her dress as she folded her legs underneath her

Rosie sat opposite her, leaning her hands on the carpet.

'What do you want to tell me?' she asked, trying to read Kyra's expressions.

'It's about Nico.' Kyra stood up and sat on the sofa, wringing her hands and biting her lip.

'You can tell me.'

'I saw him at the Carnival last night,' Kyra began hesitantly. 'He was arguing with someone. A— a girl, I think.'

'Do you know what they were arguing about?' Rosie was surprised at the gentleness of her own voice; she was usually not so careful with her choice of words.

'No, I heard her mention something about a debt. I'm not sure what she meant.'

After hearing about the Puzzle Box Maker, Rosie wouldn't be surprised if Nico's debts were what got him killed.

'Thanks for telling me, Kyra,' Rosie said, 'I'm sure the information will be very useful.'

Kyra looked at Rosie with a soft smile. 'I was with Gwydion all of last night, you know. He didn't kill Nico,' she said.

'I know.' Rosie did know. Both Liam and Gwydion's stories lined up perfectly.

Kyra's eyes widened. 'How long have you been doing this?' she asked, her voice thick with awe.

'Excuse me?' Rosie blinked.

'How long have you been a detective? I don't want to be rude, but you look quite young to be doing what you're doing.'

'Actually,' Rosie muttered, 'I've only been doing this for about three hours.'

Kyra chuckled. 'What's it like?'

Rosie wasn't sure what to say.

What was it like? She had been investigating for less than a day, yet it felt as if she'd been doing it for years. She almost always knew exactly what questions to ask, what tone to use. She knew what steps to take in her investigations, what leads to follow, what information to write down. It came so easily to her; almost like a sixth sense.

'I haven't really thought about it that much,' she said after a pause, 'but ... it's not as difficult as I thought it would be.'

'Well, you're very good,' Kyra said, smiling nervously.

'Thank you.' Rosie looked at her with masked curiosity, and for a moment, something flitted across Kyra's face. Something other than worry.

'You must be bored here?' Rosie already knew the answer. Kyra nodded.

'My father doesn't let me go out much. I've lived here for three years now, but I barely know anybody.'

Rosie knew how it felt; she had lived in Venice her whole life, but she had never gone to school, nor had she met any other children; her grandparents taught her from home, claiming that she didn't need school, because they didn't teach what she really ought to know there, and although Rosie didn't disagree, she always wondered what her life might have been like if she had gone to school like all the other children.

'It must be lonely when your brother goes away then?' she asked, distracting herself from her train of thought.

'How did you know we're—?' Kyra started, then cut herself off with a small chuckle.

'We must look a lot alike.'

Rosie nodded. She reached into her bag and pulled out a torn piece of paper. After scribbling something on it, she handed it to Kyra.

'This is my address,' she said, as Kyra took it and placed it on her desk. 'If you need anything, come and see me.'

Kyra smiled.

'I really ought to get going now.' Rosie walked to the door, but turned and reached for Kyra's hand. 'If the police come to talk to Gwydion, don't tell them I was here, please.'

Kyra nodded. 'I'm assuming they don't take well to a young girl trying to solve a murder?' she asked with a small smile on her face.

Rosie paused. 'Yes,' she said. 'Exactly.'

Then she left, quietly closing the door behind her.

VI

A BUDDING SUSPICION

SATISFIED, ROSIE TURNED LEFT out of Gwydion's house and headed for a small, cramped alleyway. The road was irregular under her feet, and the walls either side of her were dirty and scuffed, stained from the rain that constantly poured down.

There was a dulled shriek, and Rosie snapped her head up, her eyes darting. A woman stood by a window, her hands tightly clutching a baby, whose legs were dangling over the ledge. The baby was giggling as his mother hauled him upwards and held him firmly in her arms.

Rosie walked onwards, her hands in tight fists by her side. She found herself standing opposite a small row of cramped houses. It was easy to tell Alfie's from the rest; it was far smaller, almost as thin as the snaking canal that wound to its right.

The walls were dirty, the doorknob scuffed, the paint on the door chipping and peeling. There was a knocker on the door, a lion with a bronze ring in its mouth, and Rosie knocked it firmly against the wood and waited, her eyes travelling across the house in curiosity; it was tall, with an open window at the top, a large white cloth billowing in the wind. Water lapped against the wall of the side of the house which faced the canal, and a gondola was parked neatly by its edge.

The door opened abruptly, making Rosie start and look up. A man stood in the doorway, his brows creased. He was tall, with short dark hair, and a fresh cut on his cheek.

He scowled at her standing on his doorstep, as if she were a huge inconvenience to his day, and Rosie drew back a little.

'What do you want?' he asked her, arms crossed in front of his chest.

Rosie paused. There was something different, she realised, about talking to a relative; something more risky. It was as if she were treading on thin ice, and if she said something wrong, it would break, sending her plunging into a bitter pool of guilt.

'My name's Rosie. I need to talk to you about your brother.' Rosie searched Alfie's face for any signs of distress or sadness, but nothing changed.

'What about Nico?' he asked with a sigh. 'Has he done something wrong?'

'He's dead.' Rosie didn't shift her gaze. Alfie shook his head and curled his fists, pressing his lips together.

'That's not funny ...' His voice trailed off and his hands began to shake.

'I'm not joking.' Rosie's voice was clear, but Alfie continued to shake his head.

'What do you mean he's *dead*?' His voice wavered and broke, and his eyes watered.

'He was murdered last night,' Rosie said, her voice weaker than she wanted it to sound.

'What?' he stared at her, blinking, and it was clear he was trying to hold back his sobs.

'I'm really sorry,' Rosie dropped her gaze. Alfie stumbled back from the door, his eyes wide, one trembling hand covering his mouth, which was half open in shock. For a second, his body swayed on the spot and he looked as if he might faint. Rosie stepped closer but he held out a hand, taking a deep breath and closing his eyes.

'We should go inside,' he said, looking around him as if there were people watching.

Rosie followed him to his living room, where he lowered himself into a chair. He poured himself a glass of water and held it between his hands to stop them from shaking. He gestured for Rosie to sit, and she took a seat opposite him. When he had drained the glass, he placed it beside him and sat back in his chair, folding his hands over each other.

'What exactly happened to Nico?' It was as if he was scared to ask the question. Rosie hesitated. She could see from the way he avoided her gaze and wrung his hands that he was nervous, although it didn't take a genius to figure that out. After Rosie had finished explaining, Alfie was on the brink of tears again.

'I just can't believe it,' he kept saying, 'who would do that?'

'That's what I'm trying to find out.'

Alfie's eyes narrowed and he fixed her with a cold gaze. 'Why you?' he asked. 'Forgive me for stating the obvious, but a young woman like yourself shouldn't be mixed up in something this ... dangerous.'

Rosie cleared her throat and leaned forward. Before she could speak up, however, a soft voice cut over hers.

'Alf?' Someone asked from the hallway. 'What's going on?'

Rosie turned her head. A woman stood in the doorway to the kitchen, a small white cloth draped over her shoulder, dripping water onto her white frock. She pushed back her

loose plait and frowned at Alfie with confused eyes. Alfie
stood, walked over to the woman and put a comforting arm
around her shoulder, leading her to the chair he had just been
sitting on.

'Irene, I think you need to sit down for this.' His voice
wavered, like the ending notes of a violin, and he cleared his
throat.

She sat, giving him a confused glance. She noticed Rosie
and frowned.

'Who's this?'

Alfie knelt down next to her and held her hand. 'This is
Rosie. Rosie, this is my wife, Irene.' He paused, turned to his
wife and said, 'She's here to talk about Nico.'

Irene's eyes shifted to look at Alfie, who looked back at her
and squeezed her hand.

'He's dead, Irene.'

Irene gasped, holding her hand up to her mouth in the
same way Alfie had; trembling slightly, her eyes welling up.

'What do you mean?' This time Irene looked directly at
Rosie, tears pouring down her face, her brown eyes shining.
Rosie glanced at Alfie, who gave her a weak nod. She began
to explain, and by the time she had finished talking, Irene was
sobbing, her whole body quivering like a leaf in the wind.

Alfie put his arm around her shoulder and waited until
she had stopped crying. Rosie sat awkwardly, with her hands
folded in her lap. This, she decided, was the hardest part.

When Irene looked up, her eyes narrowed on Rosie's.

'If he died, why aren't the police at our door?' she
demanded. Rosie cleared her throat.

'I don't believe they've worked out the link to you yet,' she
muttered.

Irene stood up and brushed down her apron. 'I don't think

I'll be passing statements to a child,' she said briskly, pushing away her plait.

Rosie paused. 'It could be days before the police come to talk to you,' she said. 'I'm only trying to help you.'

'You're treating this as if it's a *game*!' Irene thundered. 'I simply *won't* put up with it!'

Alfie sighed. 'Irene, let's hear her out. It can't do much harm.'

Irene bristled. '*Much harm*?! She is a *child*.'

Alfie nodded. 'I'm aware of what she is, Irene, and I'm telling you to give her a chance.'

Irene huffed. She crossed her arms and sat back in her seat, refusing Alfie's hand when he reached over.

Alfie sighed. He glanced over at Rosie and nodded.

Rosie drew a breath. 'Do you know of anyone who might have wanted to hurt Nico?' she asked finally, keeping her voice clear.

Alfie shook his head. 'Nico was loved by everyone. I can't think of any reason one might hurt him.'

He looked to Irene, who sighed and shook her head. 'We only know that he owed someone money.' Her voice was dry and she refused to meet Rosie's gaze.

'*Il Signore di Venezia* ... The Puzzle Box Maker?' Rosie asked. Alfie nodded hesitantly.

'Why did Nico owe him?' Rosie tapped her pencil on the edge of the notebook. Alfie could only give her a defeated shrug.

'Sofia might know.' At his words, Irene gave a frustrated sigh.

'Who's Sofia?' Rosie refused to be discouraged by Irene's bitterness towards her.

'She's Nico's girlfriend,' Alfie said, trying to ignore his wife's resentment towards Rosie.

'Did she live here?' Rosie asked.

Irene's eyes narrowed and she muttered something under her breath.

'No,' she said. 'Nico has his own place ... she stays there when she's not with her parents.' Irene didn't even try to hide her disapproval.

'You don't get on?' Rosie searched Irene's face for any signs of suspicion, but was only met with a hard glare.

'We had an argument a few days back,' Alfie explained, after a moment's pause. 'We— I— we haven't worked it out yet.'

Rosie nodded and turned to her notebook, scribbling furiously. 'The argument you had ... did it have anything to do with Nico?'

Irene and Alfie looked at each other, shifting in their seats.

'Actually,' Alfie said, looking down. 'It did. I was running out of money to fund his expedition equipment. Sofia wanted me to continue paying, and we got into a fight over it.'

'Why couldn't Nico pay?' Rosie asked.

Alfie paused, not meeting her eye. 'Nico may be an explorer, but he doesn't have much money. He never did, unfortunately.'

'But he still continued exploring?'

'He loved his adventures more than anything,' Irene muttered, shaking her head. 'He'd do anything in the world, as long as he could keep working on that damned boat.' Irene spoke in the tone of a disapproving mother.

'He and Sofia ...,' Rosie asked finally, 'what was their relationship like?'

Alfie looked at the floor, shaking his head. His eyes were watering, and Irene's were red and puffy. They made eye contact for a split second, before moving their gazes away from each other.

'Nico and Sofia were going through a ... rough patch,' Alfie finally said. After a pause, he added, 'Sofia was staying with Nico, but she was planning on leaving him and moving away to her family.'

'Do you know why?' Rosie questioned.

Alfie shook his head and turned to Irene, who, after thinking for a moment, did the same.

'And I'm sorry, but I must ask,' Rosie continued, hesitantly, as she caught Irene's impatient gaze. 'Where were the two of you last night?'

Irene gave a furious sigh. '*As if!*'

'We were at the Carnival,' Alfie said, placing a hand on his wife's arm to calm her. She glared at him and he removed his hand.

'We ran into Gwydion and his sister. I'm sure they could vouch for us.'

Rosie closed her notebook and stood, swung her bag over her shoulder then turned to leave.

'Thank you for your help,' she said, nodding at them.

'I'm very sorry for your loss. I'll leave you to grieve.'

'Thank you,' Alfie stood and held out his hand for Rosie to shake. She did so, giving him what she hoped was a reassuring smile, then left the house.

The sun was now a thin line on the far horizon, bleeding gold into the darkening carpet of indigo. Wispy ribbons of clouds billowed with the growing wind. Pink and amber weeped into the rippling canal, fading to a dark turquoise as the sun slowly descended behind the skyline. Ravens flitted above the water in large flocks, cawing loudly over the wind. Groups of people walked by the edge of the canal, couples holding hands, or children chasing each other up and down the uneven walkway. The hiding sun caught off sparkling jewellery, sending shimmers of light skittering across silhouetted buildings. Crowds of young men and women dressed in tailored gowns and extravagant masks and suits.

Rosie stopped to buy food in a small shop on the corner. Taking note once more of how little money she had left, she went on her way.

She wondered how far the police had gotten. Had they talked to Gwydion too? Maybe they were questioning Alfie. Or had they got further than her already? Somehow, Rosie doubted it. She felt a small amount of satisfaction from the fact that maybe, she could solve the case before the police.

VII

DISCUSSIONS
AND A DEATH THREAT

COLD AND DISTANT, night shrouded Venice.
Through wispy clouds, a crescent moon bathed the streets in a milky light, casting pale yellow highlights on the rippling canal.

Bustling crowds gathered in the streets; men with tailored suits, feathers shooting out of their masks, women with long dresses and silk gloves that passed their elbows, their smooth hair twisted into elaborate styles.

Rosie spotted an old man wearing what looked like a porcelain doll on his face, while the lady that walked beside him only concealed her eyes, exposing her blood-red red lips while she talked.

She caught sight of a young woman wearing a long velvet green dress with pink and blue flowers embroidered on the sleeves, satin gloves and a light green mask that hooded over her eyes, which peeked out like shining sapphires under the street lights.

A tall man held her hand. He was dressed in matching greens with black shoes and a mask with a bird beak.

Behind Rosie, children were running up and down the

road, holding long stretches of colourful ribbon that spiralled and twisted behind them like dragon tails.

Brass cymbals split the night, drums banged in time to stamping footsteps, and trumpets drawled low, monotonous harmonies.

Lanterns hung from ropes, wrapped in coloured paper, so that beams of hued light showered the cobbles. The streets were packed with people, shoulder to shoulder, so Rosie was shoved this way and that by strangers trying to get a better look at the vibrant boat displays, the magnificently dressed dancers twirling and leaping on the decks.

Rosie turned left down an alley. The road was bumpier here, stones and slate sticking out at strange angles, stabbing dully at the soles of her shoes. The noise had quietened to a faint murmuring. A couple in the alleyway turned, casting Rosie a furious look, which she ignored as she hurried past.

There was a house at the end of the path, a dim light coming from inside, a wave of yellow rippling onto the cobbled street. The door was crooked, the window pane broken slightly at the corners, small spiderweb cracks spreading across the glass. The stairs leading to the door were cracked and chipping, the red stone crumbling when Rosie stood on it.

Rosie lifted her hand to the door and knocked. After a few moments, the door opened and an eye emerged from behind it, followed shortly by a woman. She looked striking under the dim light; tanned skin, long black hair, and bright green eyes that narrowed upon seeing Rosie.

'Are you Sofia?' Rosie asked the woman.

'Yes. And ... you are?' Sofia crossed her arms, speaking with a thick accent.

'My name's Rosie.'

'... What do you want?' Sofia spoke with the tone of

someone who didn't fancy helping a soul.

'I need to talk to you about Nico.' Rosie was getting tired of saying that sentence.

'There's not much to talk about,' Sofia said, arms still crossed. 'He's dead.'

Rosie's eyebrows rose in shock.

'How did you find out?'

'Why is it your concern?'

Rosie didn't answer, and Sofia scoffed. 'I'd like you to leave.' she said, closing the door.

'I found the body.' Rosie stopped the door with her hand. 'And I've decided to investigate. So may I ask you a few questions?'

After a few moments of indignation, Sofia nodded and opened the door wider.

Rosie stepped inside, keeping her eye on Sofia's movements. Sofia walked Rosie to a sofa and sat down beside her. The walls around her were chipping and grimy, the carpet stained and torn in places, the leather sofa worn and ripped.

Rosie placed her hands in her lap and looked at Sofia.

'Who told you Nico was dead?' she pressured. Sofia kept quiet for a moment, avoiding her gaze. She picked at her fingernails and sighed heavily.

'Remind me why I'm speaking to you.' Sofia pressed her tongue against her cheek and raised her eyebrows.

'Have you forgotten what happened to Nico?' Rosie exclaimed. She was slipping from her usual calm demeanour; her cheeks were flushed and her hair was falling in front of her face.

'If I wanted to know who killed him, I'd ask the police, not some know-it-all child!' Sofia rose from her chair and began pacing around her room, aggressively running her hands through her hair.

Rosie sighed. In many ways, Sofia was right. The police had more equipment, and easier and effective methods in gathering information. People would take them seriously, and they were faced with a lot less doubt.

Yet they had not found Sofia, Rosie had, and as far as she was concerned, that was enough.

'The authorities are behind me in this investigation,' Rosie said, speaking slowly as she tried to regain her composure. 'So I'll ask you again ... who told you Nico was dead?'

Sofia slumped onto the sofa and sighed heavily.

'Unbelievable,' she muttered under her breath.

The room fell silent for a few moments, and Rosie could hear the dulled music from outside, along with the occasional pop of a firework, before Sofia spoke up again.

'Gwydion told me a few hours ago,' she said, with a sigh of frustration. Rosie's eyes narrowed. Gwydion hadn't mentioned Sofia before, and he didn't seem like the type to hold back on important information.

Rosie looked over, but Sofia avoided her gaze.

'You don't seem as shaken as I thought you'd be,' Rosie said after a pause.

Sofia sighed. '... I'm just trying to process things.' She crossed her arms and tilted her head to one side. 'I'm not sure how to react.'

Rosie thought Sofia's excuse sounded rather forced, as if she'd rehearsed it many times already, trying to sound more convincing each time.

'I heard, from Nico's brother,' Rosie started, noticing Sofia's eyes darken, 'that you were planning on leaving him.'

For a split second, panic flitted across Sofia's face; her eyes widened ever so slightly, and her lips parted. but it was gone as soon as it had arrived, replaced with her usual glower.

'Yes,' was the only answer she gave.

'Did he know you were ending the relationship?'

Something was missing, Rosie could feel it; it was all too easy. Sofia was ready for all the questions Rosie had asked her. Too ready. It would make sense, if Gwydion had told her already, but Rosie strongly believed he hadn't done so; from what she'd seen of him, he was a quiet, anxious person who didn't know a whole lot about what he was doing. For him not to tell Rosie about a potential suspect didn't seem like something he would do.

'I talked to Nico about it yesterday,' Sofia remained calm, but there was a slight tremble in her voice, fading and reappearing, like the ending notes of a violins tune playing. 'He ... didn't take it too well.'

'I see.' Rosie could imagine a devastated Nico, begging for Sofia to change her mind, but something told her he could have been angry rather than sad. An image of him shaking his fists at Sofia and raising his voice flashed into Rosie's mind. 'Was he angry?' she asked.

Sofia looked up, and for the first time, Rosie noticed a faint red mark on her cheek. Sofia was about to shake her head, when she saw Rosie's gaze and brought a hand to her face. She nodded slowly.

'Angry is an understatement,' she started, and Rosie was sympathetic for the first time since meeting her. Sofia shook her head.

'You must understand, Nico and I rarely saw each other. When he wasn't out on his fancy ship *exploring*, or so he calls it, he was always doing something else. He never told me what it was, of course. He'd sometimes leave me during the nights, thinking I wouldn't notice.' Sofia rolled her eyes, her frown deepening. 'Of course I noticed.' She seemed to be talking to herself now, ignoring the fact that Rosie was sitting opposite her. '*It's nothing*, he would tell me,' she scoffed. 'It's always something.'

Sofia stopped talking and looked Rosie in the eyes, as if surprised that she was still there.

'It's always something,' she repeated bitterly.

'So he wouldn't let you leave him?' Rosie asked, choosing her words with care. Sofia opened her mouth to speak, but closed it again, her eyes narrowing.

In that moment she seemed to understand what Rosie was getting to. She pressed her lips into a thin line and folded her hands in her lap.

'What are you suggesting, Rosie?' Sofia curled her shaking hands into fists.

'Nothing,' Rosie insisted, but Sofia was speaking louder now, her eyes flashing dangerously.

'*Scemo*! Are you assuming that I killed Nico because he wouldn't let me leave him?' Sofia was shaking with anger and Rosie drew back a little.

'Of course not!' she said quickly, though that wasn't the complete truth. 'It was just a question.'

Sofia opened her mouth to speak, but no words came out. Instead, she dropped her head in her hands, and great sobs shook her body. Taken by surprise, Rosie shrank back a little, furrowing her brows. Floods of tears were falling down Sofia's face. Her bottom lip quivered, and her hands were trembling. She looked up, before letting out a strangled noise and continued to sob.

Rosie desperately wanted to sympathise with Sofia, but the way she refused to meet her eyes, and the dip of her lips that could have almost been a smile, made an unsettling feeling rise in the pit of her stomach.

She still wasn't convinced Sofia was telling the truth, and for the moment, no amount of tears would change that.

Rosie cleared her throat and stood up. 'Might I have a look through Nico's things,' she said. Sofia looked up, wiping a sleeve over her eyes. Once again, her glower returned. She clenched her hands into fists and stood up.

'I don't think that'll be necessary.'

Rosie sighed. 'I need more information about what could have gotten him killed,' she started, her tone level. 'And I might find something in his belongings.'

Sofia's gaze hardened. 'Fine,' she said at last, a bitterness in her tone. 'Follow me.'

She led Rosie up a small, cramped staircase. A few of the steps were crooked; others were cracked and splintering in different directions. Once upstairs, Sofia showed Rosie through a low door and into a small room.

Sofia muttered something about not wanting to be back inside, then shut the door, leaving Rosie to investigate.

The room was cramped, a tight, restricted space that made Rosie feel hot and uncomfortable. The walls were a dirty grey, cobwebs drooping from the corners, the paint chipping and peeling in places. It smelt of dust, and Rosie wrinkled her nose in displeasure.

The space was almost bare; furnished only by a single bed, a ripped lampshade, and a short table, holding a single glass, half full of stale water. There was no wardrobe, nor any place to put personal belongings. When Rosie glanced out of the window, all she saw were the backs of other houses. The rug was itchy and rough against Rosie's fingers, as she knelt to look under the bed. She coughed as a cobweb fastened itself to her hair, swiping angrily at it with her hands.

There was a large wooden chest under the bed. Rosie pulled

it out and inspected it. It was clean, with barely a speck of dust on the front. Swirling gold paint spiralled across the sides of the chest, like a twisted cloud. Much to Rosie's despair, it was locked, but after pulling open the drawer in the bedside table, a small key rolled to the front. It wasn't anything special; worn out and dull with age and overuse, but Rosie fitted it inside the lock and the lid of the box opened with a satisfying click.

Inside was a pale, rolled up sheet of parchment, tied loosely with a thick piece of brown twine. A small pile of clothes was tucked neatly in the corner, covered by a folded map with washed out images of land clumps and water adorning its surface.

Unrolling the parchment, Rosie's eyes scanned the words that were written across it in spiralling black letters:

Nico,
Give me what you owe.
You will not get another chance.

Rosie read the note, and then read it again with raised eyebrows.

Mild suspicion and whisperings of doubts was one thing, but this was something else altogether. Now there was actual evidence against someone, whoever that may be.

After a moment's pause, Rosie placed the parchment into her bag and turned her attention back to the box. There was nothing strange about the clothes, except perhaps the terrible fashion choices.

Now, the box was empty, leaving Rosie staring at its unsatisfactory wooden base. She sighed.

It made sense for Nico to have only had a small range of personal belongings, having spent most of his life on a ship, but Rosie was expecting to find something more ... exciting.

Yet when she lifted it up, the box felt heavier than it should have been. Rosie tapped her knuckles against the wood, and a hollow sound echoed from inside.

Rosie smiled to herself, knocking the wood once more. The same hollowed echo was her reply. Rosie tipped the chest upside down, bashing against it harshly, until a thin panel of wood fell out, followed by the thud of a small book. It dropped to the floor with a dulled clatter, landing on its back. It was bound in leather, with a single thin piece of cord tied around it.

Rosie opened the book and flicked through the pages, listening to the soft crackle of paper as her eyes scanned over them. The paper was old and dry, and smelt of damp and age.

As Rosie flicked through the book, she caught sight of letters, placed in strange positions, jumbled together, forming sentences that had no reason to them, or words that didn't make any sense.

There was a ring of numbers on one page, placed in a strange order, with odd, swirling symbols underneath them.

Rosie turned each page in confusion, staring aimlessly at the patterns and letters clustered together.

After several flips, Rosie found herself staring down at a sketch. It was loose, and looked unfinished and rushed. It was a sketch of a coin, one that was all too familiar to her.

It was the same coin that belonged to a dead man, and Rosie felt a growing sense of unease as she stared down at it.

Without thinking, she thrust the notebook in her bag, returned the box to its original state, placed it under the bed and left the room.

Rosie found Sofia downstairs, staring blankly at the fire, a glazed expression across her face.

When she heard footsteps behind her, she stood and wiped her eyes.

'Are you finished?' she demanded.

'Actually,' Rosie pulled the rolled up parchment from her bag and showed it to Sofia. She read the note, her eyes widening as she focused on the page.

'Someone was sending him death threats?' Sofia's voice was oddly high pitched, as if she could barely force it out.

Rosie nodded. 'Do you have an idea of who that could be?' she questioned.

'*Il sovrano di Venezia,*' Sofia whispered under her breath. Rosie couldn't help but notice how she used 'ruler' instead of 'lord' when describing him.

'It was him... wasn't it?'

Rosie's eyes narrowed. 'You know him.' It was not a question, and for a moment, Sofia seemed almost intimidated. She stepped back a little, shaking her head.

'Everyone knows him,' she said at last, handing back the note. 'And I know Nico owed him.'

Rosie rolled the paper up again, placing it in the folds of her satchel. 'How much?' she asked.

Sofia's eyes darkened. 'A lot. Too much for him to afford, that's for sure.' There was a definite sneer in her voice as she spoke. 'He must have killed Nico,' she said, her voice shaking.

'It's likely,' Rosie agreed, 'but I'd need more proof first.'

'Isn't a death threat enough?!' Sofia raised her voice to an exasperated shout.

Rosie cleared her throat. 'It isn't,' she replied calmly. 'Not unless there's a match to his handwriting, or some more concrete evidence.'

Sofia threw her hands up in the air, dropping to her chair with a scowl.

'Good luck with finding that,' she murmured under her breath. 'I doubt the most feared man in Venice will admit to murdering someone.'

Rosie paused. Sofia was right, she realised. He was powerful and dangerous, and she would need solid evidence against him, if there were any hopes of catching him at all.

'If he killed Nico,' Rosie said at last, 'he won't get away with it.'

Sofia smirked. For the first time since meeting her, she didn't seem to hold any resentment against Rosie. She looked at her, with an expression that could have almost been pride.

'I hope he won't,' she muttered. Then, as if remembering herself, she scowled again and pointed at the door.

'You may leave now.'

Rosie nodded, heading for the door.

From inside the house, the raging festivities had turned dull. The dark silhouettes of people outside were merely shadows against the velvety night sky.

Rosie's mind was buzzing as she shut the door and headed back to Agatha's house, ignoring the sudden sense of unease at the thought of facing The Puzzle Box Maker.

VIII

AN UNEXPECTED REQUEST

THE ROAD TO AGATHA'S was a long one, leading Rosie through many cramped alleyways, across countless bridges and into various dead ends. The slippery roads caused her to lose her footing and stumble, and she could barely see through the thick haze of rain. The festivities were in full swing, even with the downpour, loud music vibrated through the ground and echoed off the cold buildings. Crowds of costumed people paraded through the streets, and fireworks splashed bursts of colours against the night sky.

After a long day of unfamiliar faces, odd houses and strange requests, Rosie was glad to be back at the familiar facade of Agatha's house. The heavy wooden door creaked when she pushed it open, and Rosie cursed herself internally. She didn't want to wake Agatha, knowing she would be asleep by now. She had never been the type to enjoy the Carnival, and often told Rosie the same thing when asked why.

'When you've been dancing for fifty years, you lose the enthusiasm for such a drivel like this, Rosie. It's not like the ballet, graceful and flowing; it's loud; it's unappealing, and I refuse to take part in it.'

But as Rosie crept into the living room, Agatha was sitting by the fire. Her eyes seemed to be glazed over, and she wasn't paying attention to her surroundings. She didn't notice as Rosie crept into the kitchen to pour herself a glass of water, and she didn't notice when Rosie stepped forward and opened the door that led to her room. It was only when Rosie coughed to get her attention, that Agatha turned.

Startled, she grabbed at her cane that lay beside her. Her expression turned into one of panic, until she realised it was Rosie, looking at her with concerned eyes.

Agatha stopped Rosie's tracks towards the bedroom and cleared her throat. She pointed upwards, gesturing to the sounds of Razario's soft cries that were melting into the wind.

'Your bird never shuts up,' she muttered dryly, motioning for Rosie to sit opposite her. Rosie took a seat by the fire, watching the auburn flames dance and flicker in front of her eyes.

'How's the investigation going?' Agatha asked, and Rosie thought her voice sounded tired and strained.

'Any information worth sharing?'

Rosie nodded. 'A lot, actually,' she replied, shuffling forward in her seat.

Time moved by slowly as Rosie informed Agatha on everything she had discovered in the past twelve hours. Once she had finished, the raging fire in hearth had shrunk to small flickers of heat, and her eyes were beginning to droop with weariness.

Agatha sat back, interlocking her wrinkled fingers and placing them in her lap.

'I'm impressed,' she murmured, 'and I assume you think The Puzzle Box Maker murdered Nico?'

Rosie nodded. 'I believe so, yes.'

Agatha paused. She was holding the note Rosie found in

Nico's bedroom, and she seemed to look at it with a little more than curiosity in her eyes, although Rosie couldn't quite make out what that was. Anger, perhaps, or maybe something more complicated than that.

'Well, you'll need more evidence than this to stop a dangerous opponent,' she muttered, handing back the note. 'The police won't believe you if you show up with an old piece of paper covered in scribbles.'

Rosie sighed. 'I know,' she mumbled. How she would go about finding more, she had no idea.

A long silence followed, in which the only sounds were the soft ticking of the grandfather clock, and the dulled music from outside, that seemed to be leaking into the room, like water down a tablecloth. Rosie kept her gaze fixed to the note in her hand, and for a moment, she had the sudden urge to throw it into the fire. If she let that burn, there would be no evidence, and she could forget she had ever interfered with the investigation in the first place. She shook herself from her thoughts. There was no point in backing down. She was close to figuring out the murderer, and she wouldn't be intimidated by The Puzzle Box Maker, no matter how powerful he was.

Rosie's thoughts were interrupted by a soft knock on the door.

She sighed and stood up, sceptical of whoever was visiting at this hour.

Rosie raised her eyebrows, more than surprised to find Kyra standing by the door, her hand poised over the wood.

She smiled tentatively, and Rosie opened the door further. 'Good evening,' she said in a low voice.

'Evening,' Rosie replied, '... everything alright?'

Krya nodded. 'I have something I want to ask you.'

She followed Rosie into the hall, took off her boots, and after taking a small moment to glance at Agatha – who acknowledged the two of them, with a more sceptical gaze towards Rosie's new companion – followed Rosie up the stairs and to her bedroom.

Once upstairs, Rosie shut the door behind her and sat on the bed, Kyra doing the same with a little less confidence.

Rosie felt uncharacteristically embarrassed as Kyra took a seat beside her; Kyra's house was a well decorated, flush, elegant place, with crystal chandeliers, jewelled ornaments and gilded frames. Rosie's room was almost bare. Her bed was tatty, her floorboards were scuffed, her flowers were dying. Her house was nothing compared to Kyra's, and though she usually didn't worry about others' opinions towards her, Rosie felt a strange rush of shame. But Kyra paid no attention to her surroundings, instead staring intently at Razario, who was perched on the windowsill.

'What's wrong with *her*?!' Razario squawked, seemingly annoyed at the curious look she was giving him. Kyra's eyes widened and her mouth dropped open.

Rosie chuckled and extended her arm for Razario to land on. He flew over, and she stroked the feathers under his beak absentmindedly.

'What is it you wanted to ask me?'

Kyra hesitated. She looked away and picked at her fingernails. After a long pause, she nodded, as if to herself, then spoke up.

'I want to help you,' she said, glancing up to catch Rosie's bewildered expression. 'I want to help with your investigation.'

'Oh,' Rosie said after a pause. '... are you sure?'

Kyra nodded, and for the first time since meeting her, Rosie saw determination behind her eyes.

'I *can* help you,' Kyra persisted. 'I know I don't seem like much, but I'm good with puzzles and I know about your investigation already—' she cut herself off and looked down. She seemed desperate; she was almost begging for Rosie to agree.

Rosie nodded. 'If you really want to help I won't stop you. But I can't promise it'll be easy. It could get very dangerous, you know.'

Kyra nodded, her gaze set. 'I know,' she said. Rosie sat back against the wall. Her mind was running wild, like a pack of animals hunting their prey. She was itching to write down what she had learned.

Now Kyra wanted to help ... she was not sure what to think about that.

Rosie was used to spending time alone.

Her childhood with her grandparents had been an exciting one, filled with boat rides at midnight, treasure maps or sparring on rooftops. But Rosie had never made any friends. Often, she hadn't minded. She was at peace with being alone with her thoughts.

But when her grandfather had disappeared, Rosie was left to stay with Agatha, and life was different. There were no more gondola trips in the dead of night, no more treasure maps, no more explorations.

Instead, Agatha would make her dance all day, every day of the week, until Rosie could stand on pointe for ten minutes without fail, or pirouette thirty times in a row.

Rosie knew Agatha meant well, but more often than not, she wished she could go back to her old life with her grandparents.

Realising she hadn't spoken in a while, she sat up again.

'Right,' she began. 'I suppose I ought to tell you what I've figured out.'

Soon, Kyra was up to date with everything she needed to

know, from the exact details of Nico's body on the boat, to everything Rosie had found cramped in the chest under his bed.

'We should talk to The Puzzle Box Maker, then?' Kyra suggested, looking as if the mystery had already been solved. Rosie nodded, but something felt wrong.

It was all too simple; it fit together so effortlessly, with barely any issues. Although the easiest option was to accept that it was just that obvious, something told Rosie that she was missing an important detail.

Kyra must have noticed the hesitation on Rosie's face, for she looked down at her hands in thought.

'Do you think there's something we're missing?' she asked.

Rosie shrugged. 'I just feel as if... it's all so easy, surely things aren't this simple ...' she trailed off.

Kyra let out a long sigh and closed her eyes.

'Maybe it's just that. Not all puzzles are difficult, it's possible this is one of them.'

Rosie nodded, but she wasn't convinced, for reasons she wasn't completely sure of. Maybe she didn't want the mystery to end, maybe she enjoyed the thrill, maybe was scared of going back to her normal life.

They sat in silence, until Kyra reached over and pulled out Rosie's notebook, flicking through case notes, her head bent low over the pages, her hair falling gracefully in front of her eyes.

It was silent for a while, save for the dulled music that seeped in through the window, and Razario biting on his feathers. Kyra spoke up after a few moments.

'We should go to his house,' she said, pointing to an address scrawled on the page, with the letters P.B.M written underneath it.

Rosie nodded, scanning the neat, closely packed writing that was spread across the page.

'It won't be as easy as the others were,' she muttered. She remembered what she had heard about him, and how difficult it would be to get him to confess to anything. If he was just half as dangerous as she heard, he wouldn't appreciate any accusation against him, even if he was the culprit.

It was likely, Rosie realised, feeling an odd sense of dread creep over her, that if he didn't like what she and Kyra were accusing him of, they would likely regret the decision of asking him.

'We must be cautious around him,' she murmured. 'He is the lord of Venice, after all.'

Kyra nodded, although her face paled slightly. 'We'll have to be cunning.'

Rosie smiled, glancing over at the clock. Kyra followed her gaze, and upon seeing the time, she jumped up and scurried to the door, cursing herself under her breath.

'Father's going to be so angry at me if he discovers I've snuck out ...' her voice was shaking and as she gripped the door handle, her hands trembled.

Rosie's eyes widened. 'He didn't let you come here?' she asked. Kyra shook her head, dropping her gaze. 'He doesn't let me do anything ... he's afraid I'll get hurt, like mother— or— leave, like Gwydion.' She stopped talking and hung her head.

'What happened to your mother?' Rosie mumbled.

Kyra didn't answer, looking anywhere but Rosie, fiddling with her fingers. Rosie thought she would never reply, but she eventually spoke up. When she did, her voice trembled.

'She died three years ago,' Kyra trailed off. 'She was killed, and now— now father thinks I'm not capable of anything! He won't let me out of the house, unless I'm with him or Gwydion.' When Kyra looked up again, there were teardrops glinting in her eyes. But they weren't tears of sadness, Rosie realised, after looking at her for perhaps a moment too long; they were tears of anger.

Rosie hesitated. 'He's only trying to keep you safe,' she whispered, after a pause. Kyra's gaze turned bitter and her eyes darkened. Rosie opened her mouth to apologise, but Kyra nodded instead.

'I know,' she replied, shaking herself and opening the door.

'I'll see you tomorrow?' Rosie added in a hurry. Kyra smiled and nodded.

'Father will be at work, so I'll leave early.'

Rosie stood and led Kyra back down the stairs and out of the front door, before quickly returning to her room.

Her mind wandered back to earlier that night, when she had seen Agatha reaching for her cane in panic.

Had she been expecting someone? If she had, surely she would have given a pleasant reaction, not one of fear or surprise?

From the windowsill, Razario hooted loudly, flying over to land on Rosie's shoulder. Rosie stroked the feathers under his beak absentmindedly, muttering to herself.

'What am I doing, Raz?' she mumbled, half expecting him to give her an answer.

'Dastardly,' he croaked, although it was muffled and sounded slurred.

Rosie sighed. 'Helpful,' she muttered. She was met with silence, but for the ticking of the clock on her walls, and the crashing of fireworks outside.

Images and sounds spiralled around her mind, the same questions running through her thoughts.

For a long time, Rosie lay in bed, staring at the ceiling above, listening to the sounds of the world buzzing around her; music from outside seeping in through the barely open window, the loud chattering of people walking past the house, or the occasional owl hooting into the night.

Midnight drifted through the window, dancing round the room and settling like a damp fog. The hours passed by, and still Rosie stayed where she was, images of her grandfather's coin, Nico's dead body and the strange drawings in the old, worn-down notebook spinning through her mind.

She had been thinking about the coin for hours. She could not figure out how or why both her grandfather and Nico had exact copies, when she was told they didn't even exist anymore.

Was her grandfather lying about how many there were? There was no reason to, unless he didn't want her to know about it, but why would he? It was just a coin, a piece of metal with strange engravings on it; it wasn't anything special.

But then, did Nico have her grandfather's coin? That was impossible, unless he had known her grandfather, and she doubted that very much.

She came to the conclusion that his coin must have been a different one, but she was at a loss as to how he had gotten hold of it, if they didn't even exist anymore.

When she had looked for the coin after her grandfather left, Rosie had found the room bare; the small mahogany table and cushioned chair, the only things left inside. No matter how many hours Rosie spent looking round the empty house, she found no traces of her grandparents' belongings; it was as if they had never even been there.

Rosie sighed and sat up, rubbing her eyes. Her hands twitched towards her leather satchel, so she carefully unlatched it and pulled out Nico's notebook. It was old, with bent up corners and frayed edges. A star was engraved on the cover, but the rest was a plain, worn brown.

Rosie stared at the contents of the notebook, unable to

understand what all the jumbled letters and numbers meant. But after what felt like hours of looking, she gave up and shut the book.

Glancing up at the clock, Rosie saw that it was almost two in the morning.

Sighing, she shut her eyes, eventually drifting off into a broken sleep; a shadowy silhouette of a man, her grandfather's rough voice calling shakily out to her, and

coin-filled fields drifting behind her closed eyes.

IX

THE LORD OF VENICE

A SPRINKLE OF RAIN pattered against the window, the breeze blowing in gentle gusts behind the glass. The canal rippled and waved with the wind, the dark water billowing gracefully. A thin streak of sunlight bled into the horizon, casting bronze against the tiled rooftops. Small wisps of amber clouds spread thinly across the sky, lit up by the growing glow of morning, and somewhere in the distance, the soft caws of seagulls drifted across the wind.

Rosie chose her neatest dress; she didn't want to visit the most powerful man in Venice looking as if she had just finished a long shift of work. Unfortunately for her, she didn't have much of a selection to choose from.

The green dress would do, she decided, as she pulled it from the wardrobe and brushed it down. It was a light emerald colour, and had large, billowed sleeves, which she was never a fan of, and a long skirt, cut into flowing layers. Rosie picked out a pair of short black heels and took them with her downstairs, placing them by the door,

Rosie was surprised to find Agatha sitting by the remains of the fire, which had now been reduced to a pile of ashes, with faded smoke rising weakly from it.

Her expression was blank, her eyes glazed over, still looking absently into the smoke; it was clear she hadn't stocked it up since the night before, and to Rosie, it looked as if Agatha hadn't even moved.

'Morning,' Rosie muttered. Agatha jumped, panic flashing across her eyes once again.

Rosie frowned, taking a seat next to her, groaning at how uncomfortable her dress was.

'Morning, dear,' Agatha replied, her voice sounding as if it were a thousand miles away.

'You're very jumpy this morning,' Rosie observed. Agatha glared at her. 'I'm tired,' she stated.

She *did* look tired, Rosie noted. The wrinkled skin underneath her eyes was dark and sunk in, and she wore a deep look of exhaustion across her face.

But she wasn't telling the truth. Rosie knew that much. Agatha was hiding something.

Rosie sighed to herself as she rummaged about the kitchen for something to eat.

'What did that girl want last night?' Agatha asked from the living room.

'She wanted to help,' Rosie mumbled, her mouth half full of food.

Agatha sighed her eyebrows. 'She didn't strike me as the adventurous type,' she muttered. Rosie offered a half-hearted shrug in reply.

'And I presume you're both going to *Il signore di Venezia* this morning?' she added. Rosie nodded, brushing her hands and the front of her dress from crumbs.

'We might be a while,' she muttered. Rosie expected to be there all day at least, that is if they even left his office.

Agatha cleared her throat. 'He's a dangerous man, Rosie,' she said. 'Don't do anything irrational. I know that boxer has taught you well, but self defence won't do anything against the Lord of Venice.'

Rosie didn't answer, and instead began pulling on a pair of short black heels. She knew Agatha didn't approve of Matteo, who had been giving her private lessons in self defence for a few months. She believed Rosie should be choosing more graceful skills to master, instead of using her time learning what she considered was an 'over exaggerated dance.'

A soft knock on the door interrupted Rosie's thoughts, and she opened it to find Kyra standing outside. She was wearing a neatly cut, light blue dress with a small messenger bag slung over one shoulder. Her hair was tied into a loose plait, and she was sporting a mischievous grin. Rosie beamed and opened the door further, allowing Kyra to step inside.

Agatha greeted Kyra with a cutting smile and a dry comment about her posture, which caused Kyra to frown and straighten her back, hastily explaining that it was because she spent a lot of her time drawing, leaving Agatha tutting quietly. Then they left the house, Rosie shutting the door firmly behind her.

'How ought we approach The Puzzle Box Maker?' Kyra asked tentatively, wrapping her fingers around the strap of her bag.

'We ought to choose our words with care,' Rosie replied. 'We can't throw accusations at him and expect him to take it lightly.'

Kyra's face paled a little, but she nodded and stayed silent. Rosie gripped the strap of her bag, which held her notebook and a small pencil. She had considered taking the coin with her, but quickly decided against it; she had no proof it was even linked to the murder. It could have been by pure coincidence that he had had it on him, although she wasn't sure how that was possible. She was trying to block the idea from her mind, but it was possible her grandfather had lied to her, and the coin she saw in his study was not the last one. But then why would he have told her that it was?

Rosie didn't know, and the thought of her grandfather lying to her made an odd sick feeling wash over her.

They had caught the last of the sunrise, and dark amber streaked the cobalt sky, casting rusty reflections into the murky canal water, which rippled and billowed under the weight of the gondolas. Thin wisps of clouds turned into large slate grey silhouettes, blocking the light, shrouding the streets in darkness. Rosie noticed a woman clutching at her coat to pull it tighter around her shoulders, while a man beside her gripped his hat to his head and shivered. Above, a flock of seagulls circled, screeching to each other over the growing wind. On the ground, a gathering of pigeons strolled around, ignoring the people who strutted past them, pecking and cooing until a group of excited children ran towards them with their arms outstretched.

Tourists with extravagant dresses and coloured suits roamed the streets, crossing bridges and riding on gondolas, talking with excitement about the night's festivities. Rosie drew in a breath, and the thick salty smell of the air filled her nose. She noticed the rain begin to increase, turning from harmless droplets to heavy pellets of water, hitting the stone with an odd rhythm. She could almost taste the chill that surrounded them, bitter and sharp, and she took it as a warning for what they were getting themselves into.

Rosie and Kyra walked quickly, the cruel wind cutting at their throats like knives, the umbrella above their head struggling against its battle with the breeze.

Rosie looked to her right, noticing how Kyra was gripping the strap of her bag so tightly her knuckles had turned white, and that, although her face was set, there was a clear indication of worry behind her eyes.

Rosie's brows furrowed.

'Have you been out much?' she questioned.

Kyra shook her head. 'Not by myself, at least. This is the first time I've snuck out all day without telling my father.'

At her own words, another layer of concern seemed to cover her face. There was a moment's pause, in which she seemed to be considering herself. Then, she smiled and her face lit up, like the sun shining after a downpour.

'It's rather fun actually,' she said brightly. Rosie nodded. Fun, she thought, wasn't the word she would use to describe what they were doing.

Thrilling, perhaps.

There was something about it, the sense of uncertainty of what was to come, Rosie enjoyed it. She enjoyed the feeling of anticipation that came with asking questions and going to people's houses; the expectation of discovering new clues.

Maybe fun is the right word, she thought to herself. Maybe she liked investigating a lot more than she should. 'What happened to your parents, Rosie?' Kyra asked, her voice almost a whisper. 'I just— I couldn't help but notice that they weren't at your house.'

Rosie looked down, a hot burn rising in her cheeks, a strange prickling in her eyes that she was not used to; she was not an emotional person, yet when her parents were mentioned, there was always an unfamiliar lump in her throat, a lump that wouldn't go away, no matter how many times she swallowed or cleared her throat.

'They ... died,' she muttered, in a voice that sounded a thousand miles away, '... when I was a baby.'

'Oh.' Kyra fell into silence once more, although this one seemed more awkward and strained than before.

'I'm very sorry,' she mumbled, and it was Rosie's turn to drop into silence. All her life, Rosie had had strangers telling her how sorry they were, apologising for something they had no part of, nor could control in any way, and she had never been convinced. Why should they feel sorry for people they had never even met?

There was something different about Kyra's apology, though; there was a realness behind her words, a sense of genuine hurt. Rosie smiled to herself. Kyra was different.

They walked quietly for a while, the calls of birds and chatter of passing people cutting through the lashing rain. The cobbled street led them down many alleyways, across bridges, and through crowds of awestruck sightseers. It took over an hour for the girls to reach the address in Rosie's notebook, and by the time they had arrived, their feet were aching and their faces hot, despite the chilling wind and frosty rain that now battered the streets and canals. The morning's walk, along with the amount of running around she had done the day before, had made Rosie worn out and hungry, despite having eaten just over an hour ago.

THE HOUSE WAS AWAY from the canal, a huge, black, looming structure towering above the ground. The window frames were bent and splintered, the door pulled apart from its hinges, the steps crooked. A raven perched on the top of the rooftop, cawing sharply into the rain. Kyra looked Rosie in the eyes, swallowed, and walked up to the crooked door. She knocked three times and waited, stepping back a little as

Rosie walked up to stand next to her. After a few minutes, soft footsteps could be heard from inside the building. The door opened and a man in a smart suit and tie peered out, glaring at them over his hooked nose. His forehead was wrinkled and creased, and he looked as if he hadn't smiled a day in his life.

'Yes?' he questioned. Rosie wondered how someone could drag out a single syllable so long. She swallowed down her hesitancy and stepped forward.

'We have business with The Puzzle Box Maker.'

Although her voice was clear, to Rosie, it sounded as if a tornado was shaking it.

'And what ... business would that be?' He looked down at the girls as if they were a spot of mud on his new shoes.

'We have questions that must be answered as soon as possible.' Rosie hoped her voice would sound convincing, but instead he scowled and glared at them.

'Does he know of your ... questions?' The man asked dryly, dragging out his words in a low, bored voice.

Rosie shook her head. The man smirked.

'Then you can't see him,' he said, an audible hint of pleasure in his tone.

For a moment, Rosie faltered. Unlike other people she talked to, she couldn't barge into this man's house and demand he answer their questions, then move on to accusing him of murder.

'I'm sure The Puzzle Box Maker could handle a few questions from a couple of young girls,' Kyra piped up, her voice almost sounding clearer than Rosie's.

The smart man pinched the bridge of his nose and sighed.

'Don't move from here,' he demanded, disappearing behind the half open door, the shuffling of footsteps fading away.

Rosie waited until she was sure the man had gone before

slowly peering through the crack in the door. She caught glimpses of a plush carpet and a polished wooden cabinet with a golden candlestick on it. It was the exact opposite of the outside; instead of broken wood panels and cracked windows, there was neat wallpaper, crystal chandeliers and mahogany furniture.

Not giving it a moment's thought, Rosie stepped inside.

'What *are* you doing?' Kyra hissed from behind her.

'Let's go,' Rosie whispered back, already halfway through the door.

'What if we get caught?'

'We won't.' Rosie wasn't entirely convinced that was true.

'We have to talk to him,' she mumbled and Kyra sighed. 'This won't end well,' she muttered under her breath, as she stepped inside after Rosie, shutting the door with an almost inaudible click.

A small gasp escaped from Rosie's lips as she glimpsed the room.

It was the fanciest she had ever been in; the ceiling high above their heads was painted a crisp white, and a crystal chandelier hung from a golden hook. There was a polished oak table with six heavy chairs round it, a large bowl of multi-coloured fruits resting on an ornate lace tablecloth, which hung over the sides.

In the middle of the table, perched on a delicately carved stand was a large sphere. It looked hazy, as if a cloud were trapped inside it. Rosie leaned closer, much to Kyra's dismay, for she tugged on her arm and let out an anxious sigh.

There seemed to be something moving inside the sphere, and so Rosie carefully took it in her hands. It was cold and smooth against her palms.

She pressed her face close to its surface, trying to identify exactly what was inside it.

It looked to be an island, though the images were hazy and the colours seemed to blend into each other, like wet paint. Rosie squinted. She could only just make out two tall trees, shielding the island from the sun. The leaves looked as if they really were blowing in the wind.

She frowned, pulling away. She blinked a few times, trying to determine exactly how someone had managed to fit an image inside a closed sphere.

She turned to show Kyra, but found her at the far end of the room, pointing to a closed door. Rosie moved towards it, placing the sphere back with care.

The door was long and thin, with a brightly polished brass handle and twisted floral carvings running up the frame.

Rosie opened it, peered around the edge to make sure no one was watching, then stepped through, beckoning Kyra to follow. Closing the door behind them, the girls crept into a narrow, dimly lit hallway. Young men and women gazed at them disapprovingly from painted portraits that hung on the wall, as if they knew what they were doing and that they shouldn't be doing it. The boards creaked under their feet as the girls tiptoed carefully down the hall, their hearts thumping in their chests, their breathing heavy. There was another door at the end of the hallway, and when Rosie crept up and placed her ear to it, she could hear voices, talking quickly in low, urgent tones. Although she couldn't hear what they were saying, she knew they were speaking in Italian, though the accent was slightly thicker and more exaggerated than what she was used to hearing.

Kyra crept up behind her, mouthing the words, *'What are they saying?'* at Rosie, who shook her head in reply; she didn't have the time to translate it, and through the door, she could only hear broken murmurs and the occasional raised voice.

'What do we do?' Kyra murmured, barely above a whisper.

'I'm not sure,' Rosie whispered back, glancing behind her. The only exit from the hallway was the way they had come, and after listening to the angry voices of the people behind the door, Rosie was not particularly keen on meeting them. Behind her, Kyra was looking back at the exit with a longing expression on her face, torn between following Rosie and dashing back through the hallway.

'Rosie, they could come out that door any second! We have to leave!' she whispered, grabbing Rosie's wrist and attempting to pull her away.

Rosie didn't move. She couldn't.

Not from tenaciousness, but from fear, for she had heard footsteps approaching the door, followed by a deep voice.

Kyra's eyes were wide, and she was whispering frantically, pulling Rosie as she ran back towards the exit, which seemed a thousand miles away as they raced forward.

Behind them, the door opened, and a man ran out, shouting an angry exclamation in Italian. He was joined by three others, who pointed at the girls and ran toward them. Reaching the exit, Rosie flung it open and tore through, Kyra at her side, panting heavily.

Rosie slammed the door shut, leaning against it, her breathing unsteady, as angry fists thudded against the other side. To her left, Kyra's hair had fallen from her face and her cheeks were red. She glanced at Rosie with a look that said, *Now what?*

Rosie replied with a beaten shrug and kept her back pressed against the door.

'We get out of here,' she answered, all thoughts of standing up to The Puzzle Box Maker fading from her mind.

'Coming here was a mistake. We need to leave.'

Kyra seemed content with the idea, for she nodded and brushed back her hair.

Pulling away, Rosie and Kyra ran. They heard the door opening behind them, and the men running through. They were aware of how much slower they were, and that the men were catching up with them. But since they were so focused on what was happening behind them, they didn't notice the figure who stepped in their way, as the stretch between them and the front door came to a close. It was the butler from before, and he seemed to be grinning as he blocked them from the exit, leaving them frozen in place, while, from the corridor, the men closed in on them. There was no way out, and as they spun round, hair in disarray, breathing heavily, they saw someone step out from behind the huddle of men that shaded him.

He was shorter than the rest, but walked with determination and confidence, a long cigar held between his teeth, his hands held behind his back while he locked eyes with Rosie.

'What do we have here?' he muttered in Italian, smirking slightly. The butler looked up. 'These ... *fools*,' he replied distastefully, 'were spying on our conversation.'

'We weren't!' Rosie persisted. 'We need to speak to The Puzzle Box Maker.'

The short man chuckled drily. 'There's no need for that name,' he snapped, 'you will call me Alvar.' He paused. 'What business do two ... children have with me?' he looked at Rosie, and she felt a sudden chill of discomfort. There was something behind his eyes. something cold and unnervingly threatening, like dark clouds, warning a storm.

'We need to talk about Nico,' Rosie said with confidence, trying desperately not to break eye contact.

Alvar's face stiffened ever so slightly.

'Do you, now ...' He eyed them suspiciously. 'You'd better come into my office.'

He gestured for the girls to follow him, and after sharing a nervous glance, eyebrows furrowed, lips pressed into thin lines, they did so, following him back through the hallway they had been in.

Thick carpets shielded the floorboards, once again, mahogany furniture sat against the length of the office, and crystal chandeliers hung from the high ceiling. It could have been a perfect replica of the other room, but Rosie could not tear her eyes away from the strange objects that lined the walls and cabinets.

She caught sight of a small box with a clock on it. As she stared, the hour on the watch turned, and the lid shot open, a small, diamond encrusted bird bouncing out.

A large sparkling raven stood on the mantelpiece above a raging fire, soft twinkling sounds coming from the inside. Hanging on the wall from a thick leather rope was a pendant. It was shaped like a feather, and looked to be glowing under the sunlight.

Alvar followed Rosie's gaze.

'I stole it from a pirate captain a few years back,' he muttered proudly.

Rosie had to bite back a laugh.

Alvar pointed to the sofa behind him.

'Sit down,' he instructed. He spoke in English, which Rosie found odd, considering his accent was thick and his words heavily pronounced.

Kyra sat before she did, pulling on Rosie's wrist in an effort to get her to do the same. It seemed she did not approve of Rosie's indifference.

'Has Nico finally decided to pay me then?' Alvar asked, an

air of sarcasm in his tone.

'Nico's dead,' Rosie replied firmly. 'He was murdered.' Alvar smirked. 'That makes things easier,' he said with a small laugh. 'And I suppose you think *I* killed Nico?'

Rosie nodded. 'All our suspects led us to you,' she said.

'Well, you *are* a clever girl, aren't you?' He stood up and walked over to short a desk, pulling open a drawer and pulling something out of it. Rosie had a sickening sense of dread as she saw what it was; a long, thin knife, shining under the sparkling chandelier. He tossed it in his hands, as though it were nothing more than a ripe fruit, then placed it carelessly down on the desk.

'Oh, don't worry about that,' he said gaily, noticing the girl's pale faces. 'That's not for you.'

Rosie looked up. 'Did you kill Nico?' she asked, watching his expression intently.

Alvar smiled. He picked up the knife again and twirled it between his fingers.

'I'm afraid you're stuck at a dead end, *amore,* I did not kill him.'

Normally, Rosie would object to someone calling her "love", but since he was holding a knife between his fingers, she bit back her words.

'But I'm just as interested in finding the murderer as you are.'

'And why would that be?' Rosie didn't even try to hide the bitterness of her voice.

Avlar smiled. 'Once upon a time, Nico owed me money.' He was speaking to Rosie as if she were a child, and she bristled. 'And since he can't pay me, I'm intrigued to find out why.'

Alvar grinned drily and Rosie pursed her lips. As much as she wanted to hate this man, there was something about him that made her feel slightly awestruck.

'Why did he owe you money, Alvar?' Kyra asked, speaking for the first time. Rosie was surprised to hear no tremble in her voice. Alvar pursed his lips, drumming his fingers against the desk. He took a slow breath.

'Let me tell you a story.' A smirk played on his lips.

'There once was a man who grew up poor. As a child, he and his older brother had to beg for food and sleep in the darkest alleys and the coldest shelters. When his brother grew up, he found a job. It didn't pay well, but it was just enough for them to live on. He eventually moved on to marry and settle down, allowing the younger boy a small room in his cramped house. But the boy wanted more. He was sick of living dirt poor, crawling amongst the rubble.

'Then, one fortunate day, he met a man. And that man changed his life. He offered him funding and a job, and all the boy would have to do was to pay off his debts, once he acquired the money to do so. A simple deal, and so the boy accepted. He got a job that he soon grew to love, and made allies that would follow him into flames. The boy made money, far more than enough to pay off his debts. But he grew selfish, and refused to pay the man back. And so, naturally, the man was angry. As punishment of his disloyalty, he made sure the boy had nothing once more. Soon, he was back to working two jobs and living in run-down houses. But he still had a debt to pay, and his second job was not enough to cover it.'

Alvar stopped speaking and pursed his lips. He opened the drawer once more and pulled out a small glass. Reaching over for the bottle that sat on the desk, he poured a hefty amount of sweet smelling wine and sipped it.

'And so you killed him,' Rosie said. 'Because he did not pay you.'

Alvar shook his head. 'As much as you want to believe it, I am not the man you're searching for.'

Rosie sighed. She had no reason to believe this man, and yet something in his tone was sincere.

'Then who is?' she found herself asking.

Alvar shrugged. '*I'm* not the detective,' he muttered. His eyes seemed to narrow on her and he pursed his lips. 'And why *are* you investigating?'

Rosie hesitated. She considered telling a lie; that she was a detective, and that this wasn't the first, nor the last mystery she would solve. But Alvar would see straight through her.

'I found him,' she replied simply. 'And I'm a curious person.'

'Curiosity killed the cat,' Alvar remarked. A simple sentence, almost like a joke. Yet the tone of his voice was not a playful one. Rosie jumped when the clock gave an ominous chime, the sound only adding to her increasing dread.

Rosie glowered at him. 'I have more questions,' she stated. Alvar smirked, taking another sip of wine.

'What was Nico's second job?'

Alvar paused. He set the knife down, which he had been holding the whole time, and it was as if a weight had been lifted off Rosie's chest.

'He was working for a man named Edward.' Alvar said.

'Where can I find him?' Rosie tapped her fingers gently against her leg. Her tone had come out perhaps a little more demanding than she had hoped, for beside her, Kyra gave her a warning glance.

Kyra seemed to be a little more aware of the situation; Rosie had almost forgotten that she was speaking to the most feared men in Venice. She had let herself slip, while Kyra remained straight-backed and close-lipped, thinking carefully before speaking, if she even spoke at all.

'You can't find him,' Alvar grinned. 'Nobody can.'

'What do you mean?' Kyra murmured.

'Edward goes by many names, like I do,' Alvar explained, in the same patronising tone as before. 'But unlike me, he is scared of people knowing who he is. He chooses to hide by candlelight, using his ... minions to do his dirty work. Nobody has seen his face because he chooses to cover it. Edward is a coward.'

'Then how come Nico worked for him?' Rosie asked indignantly.

'I don't have all the answers, child,' Alvar glowered, puffing in his cigar. Rosie drew back slightly.

'How do you know about Sofia?' Kyra asked, trying hard to change the subject.

Alvar smiled thickly. 'Old friends,' he said simply.

'Did you know she was planning on ending her relationship with Nico?' Rosie pressed on and Alvar nodded. 'I was aware, yes. I suppose now she won't have to,' he laughed loudly, and Rosie flared with anger. How could he take this so lightly? How dare he brush the subject off, as if it were just a normal conversation?

'Where were you two nights ago between twelve and two?' Rosie asked clearly, ignoring the sudden urge to hit him.

'I was at the Carnival, like most, I expect.'

'Do you have anybody who could vouch for you?' Rosie asked, looking directly at him, daring him to say yes.

'I'm sure if you ask around, you'll find someone who saw me,' Alvar said calmly. He rose from his chair and paced slowly round the room.

'That's impossible,' Kyra piped up. 'Everyone wears masks at the Carnival.'

Alvar smiled. 'Smart detail,' he muttered. 'But as we've

already discussed, I am not scared of people seeing me. I do not hide behind masks and linger in the shadows.'

Rosie scoffed. Alvar raised his eyebrows.

'Is there a problem?' he questioned. He was almost daring her to say yes.

Rosie drew a breath. 'You claim you don't care about masks, but you're living inside of one. Your *palace* is dishevelled and unkept to the eyes of a stranger, yet inside you thrive like a king. You're living a lie.'

Alvar didn't answer. His eyes narrowed and he took a small step closer. Rosie felt her heart become heavy against her chest.

'If you're so focused on your ... image,' Kyra said quickly, her voice stiff. 'Why leave Nico an unsigned death threat?'

Alvar chuckled a deep, throaty chuckle. 'I did not send that threat. If I had, it would not only be signed, but I would have delivered it in person, on his doorstep, with a smile across my face. If I had killed Nico, his body would have lain in an alley, bleeding into the canal.

Rumours would have spread of his death, mere moments after he died. If I had killed Nico, people would know. And they would know it was me, and they would know I am not a man to be trifled with. If I killed Nico, you would not be standing here.'

Now, he pointed at Rosie with his knife, a crooked smirk plastered across his face. 'Because if you even *tried* to take me to the authorities, you wouldn't leave this office alive, and your body would lie, rotting in the same place Nico's had, as a reminder of what you foolishly thought you could handle.'

Alvar's face changed. He picked up the knife once more, and threw it towards Rosie. Rosie's eyes widened and she jerked her head to the side. She could feel the air move around her as the knife passed by her head. She looked over at Alvar with wide eyes, but he was grinning broadly. He knew she would dodge it. He *wanted* it to miss.

The darkness behind Alvar's eyes seemed to melt away, and he smiled.

'But I didn't kill Nico,' he said, 'and you are wasting my time.'

'I'm not afraid of you,' Rosie muttered.

That wasn't true.

Alvar smirked. 'That is a lie, or...' he paused. His voice was like steel and his gaze was piercing. His smirk seemed to grow into something more sinister, more hungry, like a wolf grinning down at its helpless prey.

'It is a terrible mistake.'

INTERLUDE

NARROWED EYES

IT WAS COLD AND DARK in the room. A single candle shed little light on the man, as he sat by the small window.

In the dim glow, his shadow seemed to be vibrating against the wall.

He leaned forward. The floorboards creaked, and the rickety table sagged under the pressure of his elbows. The flame flickered and quivered against his breath.

The man watched.

He watched the door to the house open. He watched the girls walk out and glance behind them. He watched the shadow behind the window disappear.

The man listened.

He listened to the bang of a door slamming shut. He listened to the clicking of heels against slick cobbled roads. He listened to the clatter of loose boards rattling in the wind.

The man leaned closer and opened the window.

There was a rush of cold air. The thick smell of salt. A leaf drifting in from the wind.

The man dipped forward. A sprinkle of raindrops hit his face. He blinked. He inclined his head and dropped his gaze to the ground, just quickly enough to see the two girls rounding a corner.

Their conversation drifted with the breeze, the soft buzz of chatter floating upwards. Against the wind, he could only hear murmurs and whispers.

But in the icy afternoon, leaning his head out of the window, raindrops falling into his hair, a smile split the man's face like tree roots through brickwork.

X

CLOCKWORK

THE GIRLS LEFT quickly and quietly, slipping into the street and shutting the rickety wooden door behind them. As she walked, Rosie couldn't get Alvar's words out of her head. She *was* afraid of him.

She might have lied in his office, but she had not hid it well.

She was scared of the way he looked at her; reading her like an open book. She was scared of his threats, and the way he made them so effortlessly, as if they were barely a hiccup in his plans. She was scared of how easily he threw that knife at her.

Rosie thought of the man named Edward, and how difficult it would be to find him, if nobody knew what he looked like or where he lived. Rosie wondered how Nico ended up working with someone who kept his identity a secret to the public. If it was for the money, surely he could have chosen a more practical option, instead of getting himself mixed up with criminals.

The same questions spiralled through her mind, and she barely paid any attention to her surroundings as she walked back; the buzzing of excited people chattering as they walked past, the wind whistling as it blew under bridges and tunnels, the soft waves lapping at the low stone walls.

Beside her, Kyra's eyes were glazed over with thought, and she was clutching the strap of her bag tightly.

As they approached Agatha's house, they became aware of loud shouts and raised voices. Rosie frowned. As she opened the door, the voices became clearer, more definite.

'I told you to leave! Why are you still here?!' Agatha was shouting, throwing her hands in the air.

'You don't control me,' a croaking voice replied, unbothered. Rosie smirked and stepped closer, leaning against the wall and crossing her arms. Kyra shot her a curious look, but Rosie held her wrist and pointed to the room. Razario was perched on the mantelpiece above the fire, just far enough so Agatha couldn't reach him.

'It's *my* house!' she demanded, wagging her cane in the air. He flew higher, landing on the chandelier and chuckling hoarsely. Agatha let out a loud cry of frustration and sat back in her chair, crossing her legs.

'You're old and slow!' Razario teased, dragging out his words and biting the feathers underneath his right wing.

Rosie smirked.

'If you don't shut up I'll kill you,' Agatha growled, 'and don't think for one second I won't! I don't care that you're Rosie's only friend.'

Rosie scoffed and beside her, Kyra stifled a laugh.

'You wouldn't dare!' Razario croaked, 'you are inferior.' He spoke in jagged words and broken vowels as he pierced his sentence together, though Agatha was very aware of what he was saying. She glowered at him.

'Oh, please! You're nothing but a pigeon!'

'How DARE you?!' It always annoyed Razario when Agatha referred to him as a pigeon. Of course, that's why she did it. She made sure she did anything and everything that would irritate him, since he had shredded her favourite jumper after she hadn't fed him.

'You ... simple ... old woman,' Razario returned, his sentence slurred a little.

Taking the opportunity to interject, Rosie stepped forward, Kyra following close behind her.

'Afternoon, Agatha,' she said, heading straight for the door by the stairs.

'Rosie, and ... I forget.' She gave Kyra a stern look, who unconsciously rolled back her shoulders.

Agatha smiled. 'Ah, Kyra, is it?'

Kyra gave her a confused glance and nodded with hesitancy.

Agatha grinned. 'Posture makes a large impact on how I view a person,' she muttered.'

There was a definite smirk on her face, and even Razario gave a small croak of approval. He flew down from the chandelier and landed on Agatha's shoulder. She frowned and swatted him away.

'I still hate you,' she muttered, shaking her head.

'I still hate you,' he mocked, his voice identical to her own. Agatha let out an exasperated sigh and marched from the room.

Rosie chuckled and gestured for Kyra to follow her upstairs, extending out her arm for Razario to perch on.

'WHAT DO YOU THINK ROSIE?' Kyra mumbled, settling herself on Rosie's bed, looking around her room as she spoke. Rosie followed her gaze, her eyes travelling over the familiar worn wallpaper, the cold wooden floor, the window with the small vase underneath it, its flowers blowing in the breeze.

'We must find out more about Edward,' Rosie spoke in hushed tones, almost as if she thought someone was listening to them.

'That might prove difficult,' Kyra said with bristling

frustration, 'since nobody even knows if he exists.'

Rosie nodded. She tried to think of a plan, but only broken ideas and half-hearted conspiracies formed in her mind.

'We should speak to Sofia,' Kyra suggested, after she felt the silence had lasted long enough. ' I know Gwydion didn't leave the house yesterday, he couldn't have told her Nico died. She's lying to you about something.'

Again, Rosie nodded, already on her feet and heading for the door.

HALF AN HOUR LATER, Kyra was knocking on Sofia's door, the cold wind blowing on her face, the harsh rain reappearing from behind the dark grey clouds, pattering against window panes and splashing on fogged spectacles. The crooked door opened, revealing Sofia, her long black hair tied in a bun at the base of her neck, her arms crossed.

When she saw Rosie, she sighed and her glower seemed to deepen

'What do *you* want?' she asked, not opening the door further.

'We have more questions,' Rosie said firmly.

Sofia scowled. 'I've told you all I know,' she said, moving to close the door. Rosie stepped forward, placing her hand against the door to stop it from moving.

'What history do you have with Alvar?' she asked.

Sofia flinched at the sound of his name.

'I've never met him,' she said shakily.

'I think you're lying,' Rosie said, her tone level. Sofia shook her head and stepped back, letting go of the door. Kyra moved it open, and the girls stepped inside. Sofia slumped down on a chair and crossed her legs.

'I think you and Alvar know each other quite well.' Here,

Rosie paused. She had been thinking about the relationship between Sofia and Alvar since he had uttered her name; something in the way he had spoken about her made Rosie think he was hiding something; unlike the rest of his speech, Sofia's name was announced differently – with caution, as if he were on a cliff, and her name was the gust of wind that would push him off the edge if he uttered it wrong.

'I think,' Rosie continued, 'you and Alvar are friends. Or ... maybe more than that?'

Sofia rose from her chair so quickly it fell to the floor, hitting the wooden boards with a clatter.

'How *dare* you?' Sofia demanded, 'what are you implying?!'

Rosie shrugged. 'You're keeping something from me. And, as a detective investigating *your* late partner's murder, I wouldn't advise that behaviour.'

Sofia was furious.

Her hands were balled in shaking fists, her face flushed, her eyes filled with angry tears. A red streak burned across her cheeks, and for a moment Rosie thought she might reach forward and slap her.

'Are you suggesting that *I* had a part in Nico's death?' her voice was barely higher than a whisper now, as if she could hardly believe the words coming out of her own mouth.

'Maybe,' Rosie said in the same hushed voice, 'or you could just admit you were with Alvar and I'll leave you in peace.'

Sofia's whole body was now shaking, her mouth pressed into a thin line.

'*What?*' she demanded.

On the seat beside her, Kyra shot Rosie a quizzical look.

'Oh, *please!*' said Rosie, her patience gone, 'I know Gwydion wasn't the one who informed you of Nico's death, you're not fooling anyone!'

'You're wrong!' screamed Sofia, 'I fooled Nico! He—' she stopped abruptly and sank to the floor, dropping her head into her hands.

'He found out, didn't he?' Kyra asked, and much to Rosie's surprise, her voice was sharp and dangerously quiet.

Sofia nodded. 'He was never meant to know,' she mumbled.

'So what did you do about it?' Rosie demanded, and Sofia jerked her head up.

'I didn't kill him!'

She looked defeated. All the fire had drained out of her face, only to be replaced with a sad, tired look.

'And Alvar didn't either. We were ... together on the night of his murder.'

Rosie paused. 'What did Nico do when he found out about the two of you?'

'He just left,' Sophia answered, without hesitating. 'That was the last time I saw him before—' she cut herself off and fell silent, dropping her gaze to the floor.

Rosie stood up. 'I think that'll be all,' she said, heading for the door, 'we'll come back if we have to.'

Sofia didn't answer. She turned away from them and waved absentmindedly at the door.

Rosie and Kyra exchanged a look, before stepping out to trudge into the harsh wind and thundering rain.

'How did you know, Rosie?' Kyra asked, as they turned a corner and stepped into an abandoned alleyway, the bitter wind chilling on their skin, the rain thundering against their umbrella.

Rosie paused. The truth was, she hadn't known for sure; she had nothing specific to go on, apart from the small sense that they were hiding something: she had noticed in Alvar's office how, when she mentioned Sofia, his eyebrows rose ever so slightly, and he paused a little. And when Alvar's name came up, Sofia had looked to the floor, avoiding her gaze.

'According to Alfie, Nico and Sofia had been happy until something happened. Sofia told me they had just drifted apart, but after seeing the death threat, she immediately pinned the blame on Alvar.'

'But that makes sense,' Kyra said quietly, 'wouldn't *you* blame him?'

Rosie nodded. 'Of course I would, but Sofia brought him up without me even having to mention him. At first, I thought that was just because of his reputation, or worse, that she killed Nico herself, but after talking to Alvar, it gave me the feeling that they'd met before.'

'That would explain the argument between her and Nico,' Kyra said. 'But if he'd found out Sofia had been seeing Alvar, maybe she *asked* Alvar to get rid of Nico.'

Rosie hesitated. She hadn't thought of that: that they could be working together, giving each other an alibi. But they had no way to prove that; Alvar could have paid any of his men to kill Nico. He could have been on the other side of Venice when the murder happened.

Rosie turned around, mid step, striding back down the alley.

'Where are you going?' Kyra called, as she chased after her.

'To see Alvar.'

THE BUILDINGS THEY PASSED were tall and thin, crumbling and cracked in places. Doors swung open with the wind, and windows bashed against walls, scraping the stone. It reeked of damp, old mould. and the girls covered their noses as they walked by. Having spent her entire life in Venice, Rosie was used to the smell, but her frown still twisted in displeasure as she strode past. The bottom of her frock dragged against a dirty puddle, and not for the first time, Rosie wished she didn't always have to wear such impractical clothing. Dresses and lacy gloves were all very well when it came down to evenings in parlours – not that she went to many of those – but for chasing down possible murderers, she couldn't have chosen anything more absurd. Then again, nobody *was* expecting young girls to be investigating crimes. Nobody was expecting young girls to be doing anything, in fact, except finding a rich man and staying at home to bear his children and clean his house.

Rosie walked quickly, her hands swinging by her side, her satchel bashing against her waist.

On her left, Krya, hitched up her skirt and stepped gracefully over a puddle, landing on the stone with a soft *click* of her heels. She caught Rosie's eye and smiled slightly, then snapped her gaze back to the passing houses.

Alvar's house wasn't far, and soon, its cracked facade loomed in front of them. Rosie knocked on the rotting wooden door and waited, clasping her hands behind her back.

A creak announced a large, twisting moustache, which appeared through the gap between the damaged door and the doorframe, followed by a grimace and a quiet scowl.

'You again,' the butler grunted.

He made to close the door, but Rosie's foot was already jamming it open, and, ignoring the butlers resisting shouts, Rosie and Kyra walked through the room, past the neatly arranged ornaments, the smart mahogany tables and the sparkling chandeliers.

They marched through the hallway, past the disapproving portraits and heavily gilded frames, and threw open the heavy wooden door at the end, emerging into Alvar's study. The room was empty, the red leather sofas sitting unoccupied in the middle of the carpet, the walls covered with strange, whirring objects, sparkling against the sunlight that peeked through the half-open curtains. The clock on the far side of the wall was ticking softly, although each twisting golden handle was gliding against its natural direction, as if time was moving backwards. Rosie wondered why a man would need so many clocks in his house.

She glanced over to it once more, before moving over to the door that stood underneath it, a chill breeze drifting in from outside. Kyra stepped forward and opened it further, stepping through and disappearing behind it, Rosie following close behind her.

Alvar was outside, leaning against the wall, a cigar held between his lips. He was fiddling with something, which, on closer glance, turned out to be a small, golden lizard. The tail was twisting, and every so often, its mouth dropped and a thin metal tongue rolled out.

He glanced over at the girls and chuckled dryly. Taking the cigar from his mouth, he pressed its tip against the stone. It fizzed, and a thin trail of smoke floated upwards.

'You've caught me,' he said, gesturing to the reduced cigar. 'I was supposed to be working.'

Rosie tilted her head to the side and forced a small smile.

'We need to talk to you,' she said, and Alvar chuckled again. He shook his head, muttering to himself quietly, then placed his hand on the small of her back, and led her inside, gesturing for Kyra to follow. Normally, Rosie would have brushed his hand away, but she decided against it, grabbing Kyra's wrist and pulling her in beside her.

Alvar took a seat in a red armchair, crossing his legs, intertwining his fingers, while Rosie and Krya seated themselves on the sofa opposite him. Kyra placed her hands in her lap, her back straight, while Rosie leant against the arm of the chair.

'Alvar,' she said in a dangerously pleasant voice, 'what history do you have with Sofia?'

Alvar raised his eyebrows, rolling his tongue over his teeth and tilting his head to the side slightly.

'I barely know her,' he said in Italian.

Rosie shook her head. 'You're lying,' she muttered quietly.

'You and Sofia know each other quite well. Perhaps ... too well.'

Alvar twitched. 'What are you suggesting, Miss Lightwing?' he asked, deadly quiet. It was the first time he used her name, and it felt as if he had cursed her by uttering it.

'I'm not *suggesting* anything,' Rosie fired back, 'just tell me you were with Sofia on the night of Nico's murder, and I'll leave you in peace from now on.'

Alvar stood up and walked quickly over to her. He grabbed Rosie's chin and forced her to look at him.

'I don't think it's wise for you to come here and make threats,' he muttered. 'Just because we talked earlier on, does not mean you can barge in here at any time you please, and I certainly do *not* have time for your aimless threats, Miss Lightwing. You have *nothing* on me.'

Rosie wrenched Alvar's hand off her chin. He smirked. He had seen the terrified look that passed behind Rosie's eyes.

There was an icy silence, pierced only by the soft ticking of the grandfather clock.

'Sofia already told us,' Rosie tried, in an effort to calm her sense of unease.

Alvar raised his eyebrows. 'Then you already have the answer.'

XI

SHIFTING PERSPECTIVES

Alvar didn't let the girls get many more words out, ushering them out of his office with a false smile and a pleasant warning about what would happen the next time they barged into his house unannounced.

'That got us nowhere,' Kyra remarked from beside her. Rosie gave a defeated nod, glancing at the ground.

'We don't have any more suspects,' she mumbled. 'At the moment it's between Sofia and Alvar.'

As they turned a corner, Rosie felt as if the conversation had led them down a dead end; even if Sofia and Alvar admitted to seeing each other, there was still the option that one of them killed Nico; they could have covered for each other, knowing what was going to happen, or Alvar could have hired someone to kill Nico for him, although Rosie doubted that was the case.

Kyra paused. 'It's likely neither of them did it ...'

'Even so, we have no idea who else could have killed Nico, and how to find them.' Rosie was not hopeful and Kyra could tell. She gave a halfhearted smile which turned to a wince as she stepped over a puddle, carefully lifting up her skirt, so that it did not catch in the murky water.

They walked on in silence, listening to the rain patter against rooftops and beat on windows, soaking the occasional piece of clothing that was still hanging outside.

The gondolas had pools of water in them, and the few who used them sat carefully, so as to avoid getting wet. The rain rippled the water in the canal, and as Rosie watched, small circles spread into larger and larger once, intersecting with each other as the water rolled gently up and down, bringing to Rosie's mind, a memory she hadn't been aware she still had:

It was a cold, late October afternoon and Rosie was in her room, gazing up at the ceiling, an open book lying on her stomach, one hand stroking Razario's feathers. Rain drummed on the windowpane, small droplets of water chasing each other down the cool glass.

On any other day, the rain was calm and peaceful, but today, Rosie was not calm and peaceful. She was restless, angry and confused. Her grandparents had left, and she couldn't understand why. Some small part in Rosie's mind said it was her fault, that her grandparents didn't want her anymore, and that was why they had gone, and they weren't coming back. But Rosie knew that wasn't really the case. Her grandparents had loved Rosie like a daughter, and had raised her as their own when her parents had died. So why had they abandoned her?

And no matter how many hours she spent glancing out windows in hope that she would see their faces, they never returned, and she couldn't understand why.

Rosie was distracted from her thoughts when Kyra tugged at her sleeve, gesturing behind her. She turned to hear a loud chattering.

'Laura, have you heard? Nico Lombardi was *murdered!*'

Looking over her shoulder, Rosie caught sight of two older women, walking briskly. One had long, honey-coloured hair, which she had pulled into an elaborate bun, small strands falling perfectly in front of her face. The other woman was shorter, with a dark brown plait hanging loosely down her back, complementing the forest green of her long-sleeved dress, which she repeatedly lifted over the ground.

'Murdered?' Laura asked incredulously, 'Emelia! When?'

'Just yesterday! I heard he was killed on Albert's boat!'

'No!' Laura twisted her plait in between her fingers, her eyes wide. 'Did *Albert* kill him?'

'He didn't! He was proved innocent by the police.'

'How ghastly! I suppose the killer hasn't been caught yet?'

'I'm afraid not,' Emelia was clearly loving the attention, 'but I heard someone saw the murderer running away from the ship!'

Laura gasped loudly and covered her mouth with a gloved hand. Kyra spun around, facing the two women.

'Excuse me,' she asked, 'but what do you mean, someone saw the murderer?' Emelia gave a high pitched chuckle.

'Interested in these types of things, are you?' she asked. Kyra nodded, and the two of them stopped walking to let the women explain.

'Just this morning, someone told me they saw a shadowy figure running away from the boat Nico died in!'

'Did this person say what the figure looked like?' asked Rosie. Emelia nodded, her perfectly curled blonde hair bobbing up and down when her head moved.

'She said the figure was tall, definitely a man.'

Rosie looked up. 'I would simply *love* to speak to her!' she gushed, her voice rising in pitch.

Emelia raised an eyebrow. 'What business would two young women like yourselves have with her?'

Rosie hesitated. She opened her mouth to speak, but her reply was cut off by Kyra's voice.

'You know, I was near the ship that night. And I thought I saw someone leave.' she whispered, her tone low, a tremble to her words. Rosie glanced at her with a raised eyebrow.

'And just yesterday ...' she trailed off, closing her eyes and swallowing thickly. 'I could have sworn the same figure was near my house.'

Laura let out a dramatic gasp at Kyra's words. Kyra ignored her.

'And I'm *awfully* scared, because— what if the man knows who I am, and he's trying to kill *me* too?'

Rosie placed a hand on Kyra's shoulder. 'You see, we *must* find out if it is the same person. We could be in *terrible* danger.'

Emelia nodded. 'Of course, that you must. She's staying in the Palazzo Bauer. Her name's Eva. Eva White.'

Rosie smiled, already marching off, grabbing Kyra wrist as she began to walk.

'Thank you!' she called over her shoulder as she and Kyra dashed back through the crowds of tourists, leaving the two ladies staring after them.

THE PALAZZO BAUER was a large, brick hotel, overlooking the Grand Canal. It had long glass windows, with pale stonework curving over the top of them, forming elegant archways above the thick glass. The glass doors to the Palazzo were framed either side by two cream-coloured curtains. There were tables neatly arranged below a large red umbrella, a few brave tourists sitting underneath it, despite the thrashing rain. Gondolas were moored by the entrance to the building, a gondolier in each one, waiting for passengers.

Before Rosie could enter the building, Kyra stopped her

by placing a hand on her arm. Rosie gave her a confused look and she smiled.

'I don't think anyone will answer us if we look like we were at war with the wind. Let me fix your hair.'

She brought out a small, pearl-encrusted mirror and held it in front of her face while she patted down her hair and pinched her cheeks until they reddened. She frowned as she pulled out a clip from her own hair and attempted to pin down Rosie's messy curls, only to find them springing back as she secured them in place.

Rosie chuckled. She had tried herself many times, but had always been unsuccessful. Her hair used to be longer than Kyra's, but after endlessly trying to brush through a tangled mess of curls, she had decided to chop it off, much to Agatha's disapproval.

But unfortunately for Rosie, her hair wasn't any easier to handle short or long, and she soon gave up trying. Kyra, however, had somehow managed to smooth it down, by creating two small braids and pinning them together at the back of her head.

As Rosie and Kyra entered the building, a smartly dressed man in a red and white shirt walked up to them. Rosie realised how little attention he would have given her if they hadn't tidied themselves up.

'May I help you *signorine*?' he asked politely in Italian. 'We're looking for Miss White. She ... left something with us and we must return it as soon as possible.' Rosie didn't expect him to give them a guest's name without a plausible reason.

'Ah, Miss White. You're lucky,' he said. 'She's just about to leave.' He gestured to a tall woman in a long bustled dress, standing by one of the many tables outside. Rosie smiled and thanked the man, walking over to where Eva stood, one hand on a large leather bag, the other holding a small mirror she was looking into. 'Excuse me?' asked Rosie, walking up to her confidently. Eva swung round, her shoulder-length hair whipping into her face. 'Yes?' she asked in an English accent and Rosie stepped forward.

'I heard you witnessed someone running from a murder scene?'

'Oh.' Eva looked down and nodded. 'Yes, I did'

'Could you possibly give us details on the figure?' asked Rosie.

Eva paused. Her cheeks flushed slightly and she avoided Rosie's gaze. 'You're not getting yourselves into something you shouldn't?' she asked, wringing her hands.

Rosie shook her head. 'Of course not,' she replied. 'We're just interested in your story.'

Eva eyed them suspiciously, but eventually gave a small nod.

'He was tall ... he had long hair and was holding a metal pipe in his hand.' she paused and looked down. 'He— he was running with a limp, I think,' she added hesitantly.

Rosie smiled. 'Is there anything else?'

Eva shook her head. 'It was dark, she said slowly.

'I only saw his silhouette. Sorry.'

Rosie nodded and turned to leave when Eva spoke up again. 'Wait ...,' she said in a shaky voice.

'I do remember something! He went into a building opposite the boat.'

Rosie narrowed her eyes. 'Which one?' she asked, slightly impatient.

'It was the red brick building, the one that's falling apart.'

An image of a crumbling red brick building flashed in Rosie's mind, and she nodded. 'Thank you for your help,' Kyra called behind her shoulder, as she struggled to keep up with Rosie, who had already dashed away.

Darting breathlessly through tourist packed courtyards, narrow passages and bustling streets, Rosie and Kyra made their way to the *Hope,* skidding on the slick stone, their hearts crashing against their chests.

When they finally made it to the building, they were panting and out of breath, and the sharp air cut slashes in their throats. The building loomed over them, the crumbling brick and cracked glass matching Eva's description perfectly. Catching her breath, Rosie stepped forward and extended a hand towards the wooden door. Before she could open it, however, the door swung open and bashed the stone wall behind it.

Rosie frowned, placing a finger over her lips as she and Kyra tiptoed into the building. Rosie's hand was extended to stop Kyra from moving forward. Kyra seemed to frown at that, brushing her hand away. Rosie glanced over and Kyra gave her an almost apologetic look, before turning her attention to the room once more.

It was dark inside, the only light coming from one cracked window in the wall. The room was empty, save from a large wooden crate in the right corner, and a few crooked steps leading to a half splintering platform that had so many holes in it, Rosie could see straight through the wood. She moved instinctively to the crate, reaching out a gloved hand to look. Inside, there was a pile of neatly folded clothes, a pair of binoculars, and a small bottle with no label on it.

'Nico was being watched,' Rosie said to Kyra, who was halfway up the wobbling stairs.

'What? How do you know?' she asked anxiously, glancing behind her shoulder. 'There's a pair of binoculars, and I presume the clothes are for the man who stayed here.' Looking out the window, Rosie now saw a perfect view of the *Hope*, standing proudly against the cloudy grey sky.

'Rosie!' Kyra called from the level above her.

Rosie looked up, and Kyra held out a metal rod, its bottom wrapped in a thick leather band. There was a long, dark stain on the top of the rod, crusted over time.

'You've found the murder weapon!' she exclaimed with excitement. Kyra nodded. 'There's nothing else up here,' she said, making her way down the broken stairs, the weapon in one gloved hand.

'Now we just need to find whoever was in this building,' she said as she passed the rod over to Rosie for her to inspect.

'It's none of our suspects,' Rosie stated immediately and Kyra frowned. 'How do you know?' she asked with a frown.

'Eva's description didn't match any of them,' she said simply, looking up at Kyra, whose lips were pressed thin. 'What about Alfie?' she asked, and Rosie answered within seconds. 'He wasn't limping, and his hair was short.' She paused. 'He also has multiple people placing him away from the boat at the time of the murder.'

Kyra paused. 'Then we should wait,' she suggested.

Rosie frowned. 'Why would we do that?'

'Well if he left all these things here, he's likely to come and pick them up.'

Rosie thought for a second, then nodded, climbing up the steps to put back the rod on the rickety wooden level above them. 'You're right,' she said at last, opening the door and stepping out.

'We'll wait until he gets here.' Eyeing a small cafe with a clear view of the building they were in, Rosie headed towards it, Kyra following close beside her.

XII

CHASE

THE CAFE Rosie and Kyra were waiting in was small, with a ledge on the outside to stop the rain, and long windows that were wide open, welcoming the rain.

They sat on the terrace, keeping their eyes on the crumbling building opposite them, two empty plates in front of them. They had been sitting there for over an hour, keeping their voices low and their eyes sharp.

Rosie had learned quite a bit about Kyra, and why she was so determined to help.

Kyra's father wouldn't let her leave the house alone, and she had spent her entire childhood locked inside, with nothing but art supplies and books to keep her company. Occasionally, her brother would come back from his expeditions, and they would spend evenings together in the courtyards, or go on long gondola rides across the Grand Canal. But the rest of the time, Kyra was inside, tucked in the safety of her bedroom. Rosie felt sorry for her.

Their conversation came to an eventual halt, and Rosie looked up.

Purple and yellow bruised the darkening sky.

Shadows crept around corners, darkening alleys and casting ominous shapes on the cobbled roads.

So far, no one had entered or left the building, and it was beginning to get late. There were already people coming out in sparkling masks, long, thick dresses, tailored suits and shining shoes.

A group of young girls walked past Rosie and Kyra, arms linked, talking cheerfully. Rosie noted how the three boys walking behind them stared longingly, whispering behind their intricately carved masks.

She watched as the girls entered a large, brick building, and the boys behind them walked away, disappointed.

There was music playing somewhere in the distance, and a small gathering of children waving sparkling sticks in the air, watching as the hazy yellow light faded into the breeze.

Rosie was about to get up from her seat when she heard a voice from behind her, and a heavy hand landed on her shoulder. Spinning round, Rosie saw Enzo from the police station. He was staring down at her with an extreme look of displeasure etched on his face.

'Can I help you?' Rosie asked impatiently, eyeing Kyra, who nodded, and kept her gaze fixed on the red brick building.

'What *are* you two doing?' Enzo asked sternly.

'Just enjoying the night, and yourself?' Rosie's answer was sweet, and Enzo sighed.

'That's funny.' He did sound amused. 'Because I heard you two were investigating *my* murder.'

Rosie gasped. 'Really?' she mocked, 'but, who could have told you that?'

'Don't play coy with me,' Enzo snapped. 'I've told you already to watch what you're doing. If you continue down this path it's not going to end well.'

Rosie smiled pleasantly. 'I think I'll take my chances, thank you,' she said and looked down at her open notebook, expecting Enzo to leave, but he didn't move. Instead, he stayed where he was, peering down onto Rosie's paper.

'Is there a problem?' Rosie asked, shutting her book. Enzo shifted uncomfortably, still staring at Rosie's closed cover.

'Who's Alvar?' he asked, darting his eyes away.

Rosie laughed. 'You don't *know?*' she asked incredulously, and Kyra smiled into her hand.

'What do you mean?' Enzo looked down again, 'I've nearly solved the crime, you know!'

'Oh, I'm sure!' Rosie reassured him. 'I have no doubt you're already on your way to catching the murderer, correct?'

'I— I'm not at liberty to say.' Enzo kept his eyes on the ground.

'Of course.' Rosie was enjoying herself, and Enzo knew it. He flushed angrily and pointed at Rosie's notebook. 'Who's Alvar then?' he asked again, crossing his arms.

Kyra twitched, and from the corner of her eye, Rosie noticed the door of the red brick building open a little, and a soft silhouette slip inside.

'Well?' Enzo demanded.

'I'd love to help you,' Rosie said, placing her notebook in her bag, 'but I'm simply not at liberty to say.'

Enzo huffed in frustration. 'I'm warning you,' he said, roughly then walked off, leaving Rosie and Kyra grinning after him.

THE AFTERNOON DREW TO A CLOSE as the girls stayed and watched the building, looming against the darkening sky, waiting for some sign of movement. An hour later, however, nobody had opened the door. Rosie was close to giving up when Kyra grabbed her hand.

'Look,' she whispered, pointing to the crumbling structure opposite them. There was a soft silhouette, so dark it almost melted into the shadows; a large hulking shape, trudging slowly away from the building.

Rosie leaned forward in her chair.

Under the passing light of a street lamp, the shadow became clearer to see. It was a man, slipping down the side of a building, his head darting around him.

'What's he got in his hands?' Kyra squinted to get a better view.

Though the light was fading, Rosie could just about glimpse a pile of clothes, folded under his arm.

'It must be the clothes from the crate,' she muttered, remembering the neatly packed, blue and white pile of clothes.

'Where's he going?' Kyra leaned forward.

'I'm not sure,' Rosie slipped off the chair and began pursuing the man.

Rosie averted her piercing gaze to the ground after remembering the words her grandfather had once told her;

If ever you're following someone, only watch them from the corner of your eye. They should never see you behind them.'

Rosie always doubted that she would ever need to use that information.

She continued walking, Kyra following close behind her.

It was cold now, and people were wrapped up in jumpers and scarves, their minds set on the Carnival that evening. The sun was not but a dark line of rose, reflecting against the inky waters, casting rippling colours on the murky canal. The sky had shifted to a shade of dark cobalt, though the thin clouds stayed, wispy with the growing breeze.

Rosie and Kyra followed the man through the crowd of

bustling people and out onto a thin, cobbled road, a long row of houses to their left.

Rosie held her pace back, so as not to attract the man's attention. She watched him turn a sharp corner and disappear out of sight. Her steps were interrupted by Kyra's arm as she pointed ahead of her.

Rosie followed her gaze to the edge of the canal, where the shadowy outline of the man was perched, bending over the water.

Kyra peered over the edge of the column that they had hidden behind, eyebrows furrowed in confusion.

Rosie pointed wordlessly to the man's hands.

'He's untying a boat!' Kyra gasped, tugging at her hair, which had long since fallen out of its neat plait.

'We need to follow him,' Rosie said, but Kyra pulled her back. 'Don't!'

'Why not?'

'Don't you realise what his clothes are for?'

Rosie shook her head, noticing the man leave the gondola and slip into an empty alley, and out of sight.

'Where's he going?' Rosie asked, but Kyra shook her head.

'Just wait,' she whispered, and Rosie huffed, her mind drifting to the pile of clothes he held in his hand, the gondola he had untied, and the empty alleyway he just rushed in.

She smiled. 'I need a disguise,' she said, then pointed to an empty boat, tied to a thick wooden pole by a beige rope.

'I'll borrow that gondola.'

Kyra nodded, her eyes darting around. She caught sight of a young man walking through the alley. He too was carrying a pile of clothes. She smiled, smoothed out her hair and walked up to him. Rosie watched as she laughed, cocked her head to one side and leant forward, so that her face was only inches away from his. She grinned and the boy looked away, his cheeks a bright crimson, then placed the pile of clothes into Kyra's outstretched hands. She shook his hands and muttered words of thanks before walking back to where Rosie stood and placing the clothes neatly into her arms. Rosie raised her eyebrows.

Kyra said, nothing, instead huffing and placing a hand on her hip.

'Now, go into that building.' She pointed to a small structure with its door wide open, a crumbling grey wall visible from the outside. Rosie moved a hand to resist, but Kyra shook her head.

'It's empty. I've been keeping an eye on it for a while.' 'What about him?' Rosie asked, pointing to the alleyway where the man was.

'It's a dead end, and I'll call for you if I see him come out.'

Rosie grinned and nodded, slipping into the building and closing the wooden door behind her.

'HOW DO I LOOK?' Rosie creeped out of the abandoned building and back to where Kyra stood, nervously watching the dark alley opposite them. She was wearing the blue and white striped outfit all gondoliers wear, and had covered her short hair with a flat cap. Her trouser legs were folded up at the bottom, as they were slightly too long for her, and the sleeves of her shirt were tucked in, so as not to get in the way. The only thing she couldn't change were her shoes, but they looked old enough to fit her disguise.

'Perfectly inconspicuous.' Kyra replied, untying Rosie's necklace and placing it in the bag slung across her shoulder. Rosie nodded and glanced back at the ally.

'He hasn't come out,' Kyra assured her, closing her bag and

pointing at an empty gondola.

'We just have to wait.' Rosie nodded, leaning against a column of the building they were hiding behind. It overlooked a thin canal, tall, flat-roofed buildings and bumpy cobbled streets. The road was empty; the music playing on the other side of the canal had drawn people away from the cold alleys and lurking shadows. It was dark now, and the cold wind was a knife in Rosie's throat, the clouds covering the rising moon, a few lone stars emerging onto the ultramarine sky.

Finally, and after what seemed like hours of quiet talking, the man emerged from the alleyway and headed for the gondola, untying the rope and pushing the long wooden oar into the water, guiding the little boat forward slowly through the canal.

'Go, Rosie,' Kyra whispered. Rosie nodded. Dashing out from behind the column, she made her way to the other boat parked on the water. The gondola was long and narrow, with a flat bottom and a tall ornamental stem at each end, a small padded seat for passengers and a ledge for the gondolier to stand on, a long wooden oar lying in the bottom on the boat. The gondola rocked and shook when she stood in it, the small puddle of water collecting on the wood and soaking her shoes when she put her foot down.

Although Rosie had watched her grandfather row many times, he had very rarely allowed her to try.

This meant that trying to move the boat proved more difficult than she thought it would be, and she soon found her hands and shoulders aching, and her hair once again in disarray.

Eventually, however, the boat soon slid unsteadily forward on the water.

Rosie wondered what her grandfather would say if he saw

her now, investigating a murder, guiding a gondola through the murky waters of Venice on a cold Carnival night. He'd probably laugh and say something like,

'Always up for an adventure, aren't you, Rosie dear?' Rosie smiled to herself in the dark.

Of course he would say that, she thought.

Not far in front of her, the man in the gondola stopped. His boat came to a halt on the water, and he bent over the canal, as if inspecting the liquid. Then he leant down, picked something up and let it fall into the water. It slipped from his hands and disappeared into the dark cavern below with a silent splash. With a sickening lurch, Rosie realised what he had dropped. It was the lead pipe she and Kyra had discovered not hours before. The same one he had used to kill Nico. The only thing they had that could prove he was the murderer.

XIII

DEAD END

EVERYTHING TURNED COLD, and a chill ran across Rosie's spine. It was as if someone had tipped a bucket of ice down her back.

She shivered.

Ahead of her, the gondola moved forward, sliding across the water like a thin, wooden serpent. Rosie shook herself. She couldn't stop now, she decided. She could still follow him, still find out more about him. Rosie shoved her oar into the canal, penetrating the water and pushing her boat onward, the soft sound of the ripples calming her, despite the situation. The boat ahead turned slowly through a thin canal, and Rosie caught a glimpse of his dull green eye and his mouth, pressed into a thin line.

But something about him seemed *wrong*; under the thin sliver of moonlight, Rosie saw that his forehead was clammy, and his hands trembled slightly. Frowning, she pushed her boat closer towards his, keeping a safe distance so he didn't notice her.

Minutes rolled by; the gondola didn't stop. It just crawled in a slow, nauseating rhythm over the murky waters. Finally, and after what felt like hours, the boat came to a standstill opposite a decaying building, half encased in the murky water, light green paint peeling off the walls.

Once the boat had stopped completely, the man shifted his position, bending down to grab the rope. The boat wobbled and tottered as he stepped onto the jetty and tied it down, placing the long wooden oar inside it. Then he turned, and walked shakily into the building, leaving Rosie outside, her own small gondola bobbing up and down on the canal's surface.

Waiting until he was out of sight, Rosie used her own rope to tie her gondola to the long wooden pole that jutted out of the water. Rosie peered into the other boat that was moored beside her, and noticed an empty bottle rolling on the floor. It was the same one she and Kyra had found in the building.

Frowning, she stepped inside the building.

As she entered it, the stench hit her nose, a slick dark green smell of water and mould. There was a strange heaviness to the air. The room was empty, and the floor was covered with a thin layer of canal water. The walls were crumbling, spots of white mould patching the olive green plaster. Rosie walked slowly round the room, the cold water seeping into her shoes. She could hear faint noises from another room – a soft rustle; a quiet thud. Rosie crept through the crumbling doorway and into the adjacent side of the house. In just as bad a condition as the previous one, this room was also crumbling, decaying and reeked of damp. It was empty, apart from an armchair in the corner, threadbare and torn, the stuffing falling out of the cushion, one leg broken and splintered. There were seven stone steps set in the wall, leading up to a large slab of wood in the ceiling.

Cautiously, Rosie climbed the stairs, her black shoes softly squelching on the cold stone. Reaching out a gloved hand, Rosie pushed the wood upwards.

The board lifted up, a cool gust of wind hitting her face,

chilling her cheeks and making her eyes sting. Satisfied, she carefully climbed through the hatch, finding herself on the roof, the silhouettes of washed-out buildings and the cool dark sky spread out before her eyes. Although Rosie had seen this sight many times before it never ceased to amaze her – the ominous, twisting shape of the canal, the small dots of people dancing, the cathedral looming in the distance like a palace; it was always beautiful.

'What are you doing here?' someone demanded icily from behind her. The beauty melted away in an instant. Rosie spun round on her heels. The man from the boat was standing only metres away from her. He was holding a large rusty knife, and he edged closer towards her with each breath he took. Rosie stepped back.

'I know what you did,' she said quietly, 'I know you killed Nico.'

The man raised an eyebrow, and in the cold dark night, Rosie watched as a cruel grin cut through his face.

'Clever girl,' he said. His voice was sharp and discordant, like thorns.

'And I suppose you know what to do now.' He tilted his head to one side and wrinkled his brow, which was clammy with sweat.

'Don't you?' He teased, when his only reply was Rosie's heavy breathing.

Rosie stopped in her tracks. He was right, she realised; she was without ideas. She had only begun to grasp the situation she was in; standing on a roof in the night, a murderer metres in front of her.

She felt as if her heart was beating in reverse.

'I can arrest you,' she said loudly, though her voice was shaking.

The man shook his head, as if the idea was an unamusing joke. 'You're just a *child*. You won't even catch me.'

'You're wrong,' Rosie said, trying desperately to regain her composure. She stepped closer.

The man laughed. It was a dry laugh, old and rough, like the splinters on a creaking floorboard.

He shrugged, took a step back, and jumped, landing on the roof opposite them.Without a second thought, Rosie followed him. Her feet left the stone roof and for a split second, she thought she was going to fall. Then her shoes landed on the stone. She stumbled to the ground, scraping a knee. She picked herself up and ran after the man. Her ears were ringing. She could barely hear a thing, just the sound of her own heart, pounding like a trapped lion in her chest. She was only metres behind the man. He looked over his shoulder, and Rosie noticed his wide eyes and half-open mouth. and she knew he hadn't expected that.

She grinned. Forcing herself to move faster, she dashed forward.

Then the man halted. He stopped moving. It was as if he had just run into a wall.

Of course, Rosie thought. *He has to jump again.* The man was hesitant, Rosie could tell.

'Scared?' she taunted.' The man scoffed, but did not say a word. Once more, he leapt off the roof. Seconds later, he was on the other side again, running like a frightened deer into the night. Following his steps, Rosie pushed herself off the building, her feet flailing in the air, then once again coming in contact with the stone on the other side. Rosie smirked. She was enjoying herself, she realised. She liked this.

Ahead of her, the man turned. In the warm glow of the lamp light, Rosie noticed the fear in his eyes.

'What's wrong with you?' she asked.

She wasn't concerned, she told herself, she was just curious. She didn't care what happened to him, she just wanted him locked up for killing Nico. But the man didn't speak. He just shook his head, his eyes turning glassy, his face shining from sweat. Rosie was catching up to him, but he didn't seem to care. He just stood there, his hands shaking, his eyes staring emptily into Rosie's face. Something was definitely wrong with him, she decided, and she slowly edged closer towards him.

'Why did you kill Nico?' she asked him, but he didn't talk. It was worth a try, she told herself.

'If you're tricking me ...' she started, but the man shook his head again.

'What's your name?' she asked, perhaps a little softer than she had hoped.

'R—Roberto,' he forced out in spluttering gasps.

'I know you killed Nico,' Rosie said harshly for the second time that night, and to her surprise, Roberto nodded.

'You need to come with me to the police station.' Roberto nodded. Taking a shaking step, he moved closer to where Rosie was standing. She frowned. Why was he giving himself up so easily? And why was he acting like that?

'Are you ill?' Her voice was dry. Roberto shook his head and walked closer. Something made Rosie reach out and steady him, and she was almost angry with herself. Why was she feeling sorry for a murderer?

'What happened to you then?' she demanded, determined to keep her tone sharp. Roberto didn't speak, keeping his gaze fixed on Rosie's face. Frowning, Rosie steered him towards the edge of the building, grasping at the ladder that led to the ground. But when they reached the edge, Roberto stopped in his tracks. His breathing quickened, and he dropped to his knees. Panicking, Rosie bent down to look at his face. He was white as a sheet, and when Rosie held a tentative finger to his cheek, it was like ice, even through her gloves. She remembered the unlabelled bottle in the crumbling red brick building; how it was full when they last saw it, then empty when she found it in the boat.

'Did you drink it?' she asked. 'Whatever was in that bottle, did you drink it?'

Roberto nodded.

'We need to get help,' she decided, but Roberto shook his head. 'No ... time,' he rasped. Rosie was starting to panic. 'Well I have to do something!' she snapped angrily. 'I'm not going to let you die!'

But why do you care? something in the back of her mind nagged. *He's a murderer. He killed an innocent man. He deserves it.*

Rosie shook her head, clearing her thoughts. It didn't matter, she told herself. Nobody deserves to die like this. Roberto gasped, as his body began to shake uncontrollably.

'Who did this?' Rosie asked feebly, trying to hold his body down, though she was failing miserably at it.

'Lazarus, he ...' Roberto's terrified voice was fading.

'Lazarus?' Rosie repeated. 'Who's Lazarus?'

But Roberto didn't answer. He had stopped shaking, his eyes turned glassy, his mouth dropped open slightly, and a short, trembling breath left his lips.

He was gone.

Somewhere not so far in the distance, fireworks went off, a sharp burst of colour in the sky, illuminating two silhouettes on the rooftop.

One, kneeling on the ground, bending over the other, who was lying unnaturally still on the cold, wet stone.

XIV

COLD LIKE A KNIFE

THE NIGHT SUNK ITS COLD TALONS into Rosie's skin. Her breath puffed out in soft white clouds, and her gloved hands were shaking. She hadn't moved from her position on the roof.

No matter how many times she willed herself to move, Rosie could not leave. Over and over, her own mind pestered her to get up and run, yet over and over, she shut those thoughts away.

You don't even like him, the voice in the back of her head told her. *You hate him. He killed Nico, or don't you remember that? And what about Kyra? She's all alone down there; what if she needs help?*

After a few moments, Rosie slipped her gloved hands into Roberto's pockets, feeling around with care. When she had found Nico, the idea of rifling through a dead man's pockets didn't occur to her as terrifying. Invasive, perhaps, but she hadn't the time to think about it. Now, however, things felt different, almost risky, as if Roberto would wake at any moment and grab her wrist. But he wouldn't. He was truly gone, and although Rosie never cared for him, she felt a sudden rush of sadness.

Carefully, she pulled out a small folded piece of paper from his pocket. There was a single word written on it and it echoed through Rosie's mind:

Lazarus.

Rosie blinked in the cold air, the breeze stinging her eyes. Who was Lazarus? Was he the one who poisoned Roberto? And why might he had done so? Had he wanted Nico alive? Was he angry at Roberto for murdering him? And why had Roberto killed him in the first place?

Her mind buzzed with unanswered questions, and inklings that all her suspicions had only been partly correct.

She shivered.

After a few moments of sitting next to Roberto's body, lying cold and motionless on the stone rooftop, she stood. But when she moved, she heard a voice, and the faint sound of footsteps drawing nearer. She could just make out three shapes in the pitch darkness.

'There she is!' Rosie heard a voice say, and the pounding rhythm got louder and louder.

'Good evening, Miss Lightwing,' someone said. Looking up, she saw Enzo and two other policemen standing in front of her, a pair of handcuffs in Enzo's hand, the man behind him holding a long metal bar. Rosie froze, one hand hovering above Roberto's dead body, the other tightly holding the crumpled piece of paper she'd found in his pocket. Her mind spun, and for a moment, she considered running. If she was quick enough, perhaps she could get away. If she kept running, perhaps they would give up.

Enzo smiled smugly, 'I thought you said you weren't a murderer.'

'I'm not.' Rosie's voice was smooth, although her heart was pounding in her chest, an animal in a cage, willing to get out.

The two men behind Enzo narrowed their eyes and tightened their mouths into thin lines. One of them crouched down beside Roberto's body, placed a finger on his neck, then turned back to Enzo with a firm nod. Enzo tilted his head to the side.

'Then what are you doing next to a *dead body?*' he asked drily.

'I didn't kill him!' Rosie exclaimed, rising to her feet. 'He was poisoned.'

Enzo smirked, twirling the handcuffs between his fingers. 'And how could you *possibly* know that?' he asked quietly.

Rosie hesitated. 'I saw him,' she said, 'he just ... dropped.'

Enzo laughed dryly and muttered to himself, taking a small step forward. Rosie backed away.

'Miss Lightwing, you are under arrest for murder. Please come with me back to the office.'

Rosie shook her head. 'I didn't kill him!' she exclaimed loudly. 'And I'm not going back with you.'

'You don't have a choice,' the man behind Enzo said, but Rosie shook her head again.

'I'm not the one to blame for his murder.'

'Then why were you with him in the first place?' Enzo demanded, his voice rising slightly.

Again, Rosie hesitated. Would Enzo believe her if she told him the truth? She strongly doubted it, but something told her it wouldn't be best to lie, having been found at a second crime scene.

'He killed Nico,' she said steadily, crossing her arms. 'I have proof.'

Enzo laughed. 'I'm sure you do,' he mocked, stepping forward. He was talking to her as if she were his disobedient daughter, and Rosie drew back.

'I'm not guilty!' she persisted, her hands trembling, her

words coming out shakier than she had hoped.

'Put your hands in front of you, Miss,' Enzo said, stepping slowly towards her, as if he were taming a wild animal.

Rosie scowled. 'You can't arrest me,' she muttered, doubting herself as Enzo's cold handcuffs closed around her wrist. 'I didn't kill anyone.'

Enzo said nothing; he just dragged her beside him as he walked back to the police office, his face set.

As Rosie was being pulled along, she could have sworn she saw two coat tails, disappearing into the shadows opposite her.

INTERLUDE

A SPY IN THE DARKNESS

*I*T WAS COLD.

The night air around him was stiff, as if it were frozen solid. He breathed out, and a cloud of white faded into the sky.

The man stood straight, his hands in his pockets, his collar shielding his face from the harsh gusts of wind that rattled loose boards and made flags billow. The stone underneath his feet was slippery with rain; the buildings to either side of him dirty and old.

In the courtyards, music blared, and crowds of people filed in and out of buildings, chattering loudly over the thrashing wind. Under the hazy street lamps, jewels glittered and cufflinks sparkled. Cheery voices cut through the low, drawling music, and fireworks snapped and crackled, sending bursts of red and emerald skittering across an indigo sky.

Down below, all was peaceful and content. But the man was neither peaceful nor content. For, opposite him, on the roof of an old, torn down building, two silhouettes rested on the stone. One was very clearly dead, lying motionless on the slick rock. The other was smaller, kneeling over the body.

Although the man couldn't see her, he could picture her expressions to a point; eyes wide, lips parted, hands shaking.

The man stepped closer, the heel of his shoe making a neat clicking sound on the roof. He pushed back his coat, and in the thin sliver of moonlight, the hilt of a knife glinted.

The sound of multiple footsteps attracted the man's attention, and he moved backwards a step, to lurk in a shadow that half-encased the roof.

He heard raised voices, and saw the girl stand up and take a trembling step backwards.

The man raised his eyebrows when he saw the officer draw a pair of handcuffs from his coat. A smirk spread across his face when the girl backed away, holding her hands in front of her.

The man's eyes travelled to the body on the roof. He found it intriguing how one could go from living to dead in a matter of seconds, with neither warnings nor goodbyes.

Just hours ago, that man had been walking briskly through crowds of people, shoving his way across Venice. Now, he lay on the stone, lifeless and cold, and a girl who had not killed him was moments away from being arrested for it.

But the man did not step closer. He did not exclaim when the officer tightened his handcuffs around the girl's wrists.

He did not deny her involvement or claim to have seen the man drop dead of his own accord.

He did nothing to help, and slowly, she was dragged away.

Instead, a smirk played across his face, and he took a further step backwards, merging deeper into the shadows.

The girl was walking into something she could not understand. He believed she would get nowhere, but that was quite the opposite.

She had gotten far closer to the truth than he was comfortable with, and he was beginning to believe there was only one way to stop that.

As she was led away in handcuffs, the man nodded to himself.

It was for the best.
She was beginning to get in his way.
And he didn't like it when people got in his way.

XV

HANDCUFFS AND HAIRPINS

THE NIGHT WAS MENACING as Rosie and Enzo arrived at
the police office, the moon shining through the clouds,
the stars hazy. Of course, the festivities were still in full swing;
sparklers and fireworks lit the streets, catching on jewellery
and sequins, and small gemstones encrusted into masks and
clothes. Music still played from the courtyards and squares,
and people gathered around to watch the dancers twirl and
spin, their bodies moving gracefully. Rosie had tried to keep an
eye out for Kyra, but had not seen her anywhere. She suspected
she had gone home, or had caught sight of the policemen and
made a run for it. Rosie couldn't blame her.

The office was bustling. In one corner, a large stocky man
dragged two people in brightly coloured costumes through
a door, grumbling under his breath. In another, a woman
dressed in a sparkling gown was complaining to a man about a
lost pair of earrings, her voice loud and shrill.

As she stepped into Enzo's office, Rosie wished she had
never set foot on that boat, never started investigating in the
first place.

He gestured for Rosie to sit. She did so, placing her cuffed hands in her lap.

'Wait here while I bring in a colleague.' He looked down at her disapprovingly. 'You won't be let out so quickly this time, Miss Lightwing.'

The moment the door slammed shut, Rosie jumped up from her chair. She needed something to take off her handcuffs.

The room was dimly lit, but Rosie couldn't escape the feeling of darkness that seemed to encase her.

She glanced frantically for something to help her escape, but was met with nothing but the table and a dirty window. *A window.* Smiling, Rosie stuck her head to the glass and peered out. In the darkness she could make out the silhouettes of rapidly moving figures, and a thin alleyway leading away from the building.

Perfect.

Now all she needed was to take off her handcuffs. Rosie pulled a pin from her hair, bent it and twisted it into the lock, turning one side, while she angled the other underneath. The metal was cold against her skin, the cuffs digging sharply into her wrists. She winced each time the icy metal pressed against her, as she fumbled about the lock with shaking hands silently apologising to her grandfather, for ever neglecting the skills he had taught her.

Rosie felt as if her heart was trying to escape from her chest, thrashing harshly against her ribs.

Time seemed to slow as she scrabbled with the cuffs.

What had once been a quiet confidence had now turned into a sick sense of doubt, persisting that there was no way of escape. Rosie ignored those feelings with everything she had in her, as eventually, the cuffs clicked open and fell to the floor with a clatter.

She winced at the sound, praying that no one had heard.

Then, opening the window, she clambered out, dropping onto the cobbles with a thud. She stood, brushed down her dress, which was now muddy and ripped, then ran. Her boots thundered on the stone pathways, echoing loudly as she tore through the streets, bashing into people when she raced into the crowds.

'Hey!' someone exclaimed. 'Watch where you're going!'

Rosie didn't stop to apologise; she just continued running, her breath catching in her throat, the cold air icy against her cheeks, the music and voices nothing but a blur in her ears as she sped past.

Enzo must have figured out she had fled, she thought. He was probably coming after her right now. She'd have to be careful. Running away from the police after being charged with murder was a serious problem.

Rosie winced at the thought as she ran on.

She didn't know where she was going, only that she needed to put as much distance between her and Enzo as possible. After a few minutes, she came to a stop outside Agatha's house. There was a dim light coming from one of the windows, a soft shadow of someone pacing inside. Frowning, Rosie pressed her face to the window, peering through the glass. Agatha was sitting in her rocking chair, her hands folded over her lap. But there was a man walking back and forth. He wore a black uniform, a heavy frown, and a pair of shining handcuffs tied to his belt.

XVI

QUIET, BUT NOT ALONE

ROSIE WATCHED as Agatha rose from her chair and faced the policeman. Even from his silhouette, she knew the man was scared. Smirking, Rosie watched as Agatha jabbed a finger into the man's chest until he backed away slowly.

Rosie heard Agatha's thundering voice from outside.

'I told you already, Rosie is not a criminal!'

The policeman stepped backwards, his back arching away from her as he stumbled up against a wall. He cleared his throat and walked toward the door.

'I'm not saying I believe you,' Rosie could hear faintly through the glass. 'I will be keeping a guard outside your door in case your criminal student decides to show her face.'

At that, he nodded to Agatha grimly and opened the door. Rosie ducked behind the corner of the building as he walked past, watching as he strode away through the crowd. For a moment, she considered going to talk to Agatha, but quickly decided against it. She didn't want her to get involved, and she couldn't risk being seen by an officer. Sighing, she trudged away from the house.

Though Rosie didn't notice, the soft silhouette of a large

bird leapt from the windowsill and followed her hesitant steps, flying high above her in the cool breeze.

The night seemed colder now. The wind sliced harshly; the shadows loomed. Rosie had long since ruled out going to Kyra's house, not wanting to land her in any trouble if she could help it.

Rosie continued through the crowd of people, letting the fireworks and tinted lanterns light her way.

Occasionally, she saw an officer, and she quickly sucked into an alley, holding her breath until he had passed.

Through gatherings and alleyways, Rosie wandered endlessly, without a proper clue where to go.

Her eyelids fluttered closed, and she had to force herself to open them again so that she didn't walk straight into the canal, although that didn't seem like such a bad idea at that moment.

Raised voices and loud cheers caught Rosie's attention, and she turned a corner, keeping her head low.

The cheers got louder, and Rosie found herself outside a crowd of people with fists in the air, shouting loudly. Rosie pushed herself through the crowd to find two men in the middle, shoving each other and throwing unsteady punches. Rosie sighed and turned her back to the fight, her head pumping. Normally, the riot would have caught her attention and she would have stayed to watch. But she didn't have the time now. She used to want to be the one fighting, just to show people that a girl could be good at that. She *was* good at that, she thought to herself. She had been told so, many times, after beating her teacher when she had sparred with him.

Rosie smiled into the darkness as an idea formed in mind. She dashed through the crowd, heading with determined footsteps for the Rialto Bridge. Her boots echoed on the stone floor as she ran across the bridge, passing kissing couples, and children playing tag, sparklers in their hands, fizzing into the air as they dashed by. The chill wind flushed against Rosie's face, light rain landing on her cheeks. She brushed it away and kept on running, keeping her head low when she saw an officer standing a few feet away from the bridge. Emerging from the end of a darkened alleyway, Rosie came across a house. Light streamed out from a set of windows, rippling against the slick cobbles as she approached it.

As she hesitated for a moment, Rosie felt unbearably aware of herself, aware of the fact that she was alone at night, in a secluded area of town, aware of the trouble she was in with the police, of the second murder that had just occurred, and that she was now completely out of evidence. She was aware of her feet itching in her shoes, and her gloves scratching against her fingertips. She was aware of the unsteadiness of her breathing, coming out as short gasps. She was aware of her stinging eyes and the mould of her tongue against the roof of her paper-dry mouth.

Rosie reached a trembling hand to the door and knocked twice, as she stood, waiting in silence.

The door opened a few moments later, and someone peered out, gazing down at her with dark brown eyes.

Matteo was a boxer, and he had been giving Rosie private lessons for a couple of months, after watching her stand up to a particularly insistent young man.

And had offered her the chance to learn from him, and after almost no hesitation, she had accepted.

And now, nearly three months later, she was outside his house, waiting nervously for him to open the door.

Rosie almost jumped when he did so, as if she was surprised to see him at his own doorstep, as if she hadn't sturned up there in the middle of the night with shaking hands and bedraggled hair.

Matteo frowned at her. 'Rosie?'

She opened her mouth to explain, but for a moment no words came out, and she could only muster a trembling breath. Matteo's eyebrows creased, and he stepped away from the door.

'You look freezing. Let's get you inside.'

Rosie nodded, muttering an almost inaudible, 'thank you,' as he placed an arm around her shoulders and guided her in.

A wave of warmth hit Rosie's face as Matteo shut the heavy door behind them. A fire was burning in the hearth, flames dancing and flickering above the ashes, that gave occasional bursts of hot sparks. Landscapes and portraits crowded the wallpaper, hanging solemnly against the deep red. Two red sofas sat opposite the crackling fire, laden with cushions. Matteo gestured for Rosie to do the sit, before wrapping a thick blanket around her shoulders. Rosie thanked him with a warm smile as he sat opposite her.

Matteo opened his mouth to speak, but was interrupted by the sound of soft footsteps padding into the room. Rosie looked up to see a young man. He looked about her age, perhaps a little older, and wore an expression of confusion as he saw her on the sofa, a blanket wrapped around her shivering shoulders.

'*Chi è questo?*' He asked. His voice was clear and smooth, like a cloudless sky, and Rosie felt heat rising to her cheeks at the sound of it.

Matteo looked between Rosie and the boy.

'Rosie is a student of mine,' he muttered. 'Rosie, this is my son, Luca.' He gestured between the two of them.

Luca frowned at her for a moment, then smiled and ran a

hand through his curly hair.

He looked almost exactly like his father, aside from his eyes, which, instead of a sharp blue, were a swirling mixture of gunmetal and ash.

Rosie smiled back pleasantly and nodded at him, trying to ignore the sudden flush to her cheeks.

'Nice to meet you.' She extended her hand and he shook it, his grey eyes flashing. Rosie looked down.

'What brings you here at this time of night, Rosie?' Matteo asked, as Luca sat on the edge of the sofa, intertwining his fingers.

Rosie closed her eyes. 'I need your help,' she muttered.

With a confused look, Matteo nodded, and Rosie continued with her story.

By the time she was finished, her mouth was dry and her voice hoarse. She looked up to see both Matteo and Luca gazing at her with a look that could have almost been amusement, but consisted mainly of concern.

'What you're meaning to tell me ... is that you're solving a murder?' Luca murmured quietly.

'Yes,' Rosie said, 'and I already know who killed Nico; I just don't have any proof.'

'That and the fact that your killer is dead.' Matteo added, stroking the stubble on his chin in thought.

'And you're on the run from the police?' he continued, and Rosie nodded tentatively. 'Unfortunately,' She shook her head in disappointment.

'Looks like you've got yourself in trouble.' Rosie was surprised at how unvexed he was by everything she had told him.

'Where do you think Kyra is now?' he asked, tapping one thumb against another.

Rosie shrugged. 'If she didn't get caught, I suspect she's with her brother. Or speaking to Agatha.'

At both Luca and Matteo's confused expression, she added, 'my landlady.'

Matteo nodded and stood up. 'We can continue this in the morning, but for now we all should get some sleep. I think it's decided that you'll stay here. Luca will show you to the spare room.'

Rosie nodded. Her weariness had caught up to her, her eyelids heavy, her head pounding.

'Follow me,' Luca muttered, and Rosie gratefully tagged along behind him up the stairs.

'Here,' Luca said, at the top of the stairs, gesturing to an open door. 'You can stay here as long as you need to.' 'Thank you,' Rosie said gratefully, stepping inside the room and sitting down on the bed.

Luca muttered a quick but quiet goodnight, before shutting the door, his footsteps disappearing down the stairs. There was a small bathroom to the back of the room, in which Rosie hastily washed her face, then undressed and got into bed. Her hands were shaking slightly, as she pulled the covers to her chin and closed her eyes.

The soft murmurs of conversation from downstairs drifted into the room, and the sounds of fireworks and faraway music distracted her from her overwhelming tiredness.

She had hoped to fall asleep quickly, but of course, her mind was filled with questions from the investigation. What could she do now? She had nothing to prove Roberto was a murderer, and even so, the police wouldn't do anything about it. Who was Lazarus? And what happened to Kyra? Although Rosie suspected her to go home, it was possible she was still looking for her, or perhaps gotten herself into trouble. Rosie's mind buzzed, and she closed her eyes, trying to block away her thoughts.

Music drifted through the half open window, the slow, low drawl putting her on edge. She shook herself and closed her eyes again, willing herself to drift off. She lay there for hours, her eyes scanning over the room, though she could barely see in the air of darkness.

The blankets scratched against her skin and the pillow under her head had long lost its comfort. She sighed and turned around, squeezing her eyes shut and finally drifting into an uneasy, restless sleep.

INTERLUDE

A WATCHFUL SHADOW

I*T WAS COLD in the small alleyway.*
Half-hidden by a dark shadow, the man waited. He leaned against the wall, the uneven, bumpy stone cold against the back of his coat.

Opposite him, a window opened, and a figure jumped out, landing on the stone with a quiet thud.

The man leaned closer. It was difficult to identify the figure, but as she looked up, a street lamp illuminated her face; eyebrows creased, hair bedraggled and messy, clothes ragged.

The man's eyes widened.

He thought he had finally gotten rid of her, that the police would have done their jobs properly, and that he would not have to take extra precautions to keep her out of his way.

She stumbled to her feet and raced down the road, tripping a little on the bumpy surface of the street.

The man sighed and stepped forward, following behind her. His steps were calm and calculated, his hands thrust deep inside his pockets, his face set.

Ahead of him, the girl tore through gathering crowds and stumbled down alleyways, unaware of him following close behind her.

The man watched as she came to a standstill opposite a crowd of people, who had created a ring around two men. They grunted and shoved at each other, throwing punches and curses around. The girl sighed and turned away, and for a split second, the man thought she would see him. But she had looked down before their eyes met, and he continued to walk behind her.

Her movements were beginning to get more sluggish. She moved slower and with less agility as she had earlier that night. She turned a corner, then came to a halt in her tracks. The man ducked behind a wall, just quick enough to see her turn around and run past him.

He frowned, but picked up his pace and began to follow her. She moved into a dimly lit alley, where shadows curled up buildings and shrouded the road in darkness. Her worn-down heels slipped and skidded on the ground as she approached a building.

It was an old, red-brick house, with two windows on either side of a large wooden door and three stone steps leading to its entrance.

The girl knocked and waited, and after a short moment, the door opened, and a man stood behind it. He gave the girl a confused look, but let her inside. The door closed, blocking the man's view of the girl.

The man hissed in annoyance.

He believed she was nothing but a pawn in his chess game, and the problem of her interfering with his business was over.

He was wrong.

He shouldn't have underestimated her.

But no matter, he thought, as he turned away from the house. There were plenty of other ways to get rid of her.

XVII

EYES AT THE WINDOW

A SOFT KNOCK ON THE DOOR shook Rosie from her disturbed sleep, and she sat up, rubbing her eyes with the back of her hand.

'Rosie?' Luca called from outside. 'Are you awake?'

'I am now.'

The door opened hesitantly. 'May I come in?'

Rosie nodded.

He entered, his feet padding quietly on the carpet.

Rosie chuckled at his awkwardness and he gave her a small smile, running a hand through his hair.

'There's breakfast downstairs,' Luca said. ' ... And father's gone out for the morning ... he won't be back till later.'

Rosie nodded and gestured at the door, but Luca didn't move from his position. Instead, he opened his mouth to speak, but quickly shut it again. She frowned.

'What are you not telling me?' she asked in a quiet voice. Once again, Luca seemed at a loss for words. He took a small breath and shook his head.

'Come downstairs. You ought to see for yourself,' he muttered, then left without another word, shutting the door quietly behind him.

Rosie frowned at him, but nodded and changed into her clothes. Noticing with a faint heart how muddy and torn her dress had become, she hurried downstairs.

She found Luca sitting at the table, a newspaper in his hand, his brow creased. He looked up at her and gestured for her to sit opposite him, away from the window. She frowned at him and he handed her the newspaper, muttering only a small, 'take a look.'

Rosie took the paper from him with furrowed eyebrows.

QUINDICENNE ACCUSATO DI OMICIDIO

ROSIE LIGHTWING, a fifteen-year-old girl, was discovered at the scene of two murders, and though she continuously claims not to have committed them, all evidence points to the fact that she is guilty.

'Miss Lightwing was released when we did not have enough evidence linking her to the first crime. But she will not be let off a second time,' detective Enzo Trather stated.

'She escaped from police custody and is now on the run. If you see her, you must contact the authorities immediately.'

Detectives are still on the lookout. Rosie continues to protest her innocence; police think otherwise, and they will stop at nothing to arrest her.

The article continued, but Rosie had read enough.

'Now I can't go anywhere without risking arrest,' she muttered with an annoyed sigh, as her body sagged in her chair.

Luca nodded and pointed to the bottom of the page.

'And everyone knows what you look like now.'

She peered closer. He was right – there was a sketch of Rosie, with the word **PERICOLOSO** spelled out in large black letters.

'I must say, they could have done a better job with that drawing.' Rosie held it up next to her face for comparison. 'Do you think I look even remotely like this?'

Luca chuckled and tossed a grape into his mouth. 'Too bad. You'll be stuck here with me and Father.'

Rosie was about to make a witty comment that would probably have been slightly offensive, when there was a knock at the door.

Frowning, Luca stood and gestured for Rosie to stay where she was. She sighed and sat back in her seat, already annoyed at how little she was able to do.

Luca opened the door and frowned.

'May I help you?' he asked and Rosie heard a familiar British voice reply.

'Sorry to disturb you. My name's Kyra.' Rosie smiled and jumped out her seat, while Luca opened the door wider for Kyra to come inside, waiting as she took off her boots, which were slightly soggy and dripping water from the puddles outside.

'I have good news,' she said, as she took a seat beside Rosie. Her announcement, however, was soon cut short by three short taps on the window.

Rosie frowned and stood up, but was stopped from her movements by Luca's arm, as he moved back over to her. She glared at him.

'It could be someone who's come looking for you,' he muttered. Her scowl only increased, but she sat down and crossed her arms in a huff.

Luca approached the window. He had been expecting to

see someone peering through the glass, but was greeted instead by a pair of beady black eyes, and a hooked beak. He jumped back a little, caught off guard, cursing under his breath.

Rosie, who had leaned over the table to get a better look, despite Kyra tugging on her sleeve and rolling her eyes, had caught sight of Razario, tapping his beak increasingly faster and more impatiently on the glass. She moved over and opened the window, and Razario flew straight to her, landing on her shoulder.

She smiled and stroked the feathers under his chin.

'How did you find Rosie?' Luca asked, directing his question at Kyra.

'I talked to Agatha,' Kyra replied quietly, 'she mentioned where you live.'

'Were you followed?' Rosie questioned.

Kyra shook her head. 'I took a long, winding route and hid my face to make sure I wasn't.'

Rosie nodded in thanks and went back to her slice of toast, while Luca filled up a glass of water and handed it to Kyra, who accepted it with a smile.

'What did *you* discover?' Kyra asked.

'Death and treachery,' squealed Razario. Everyone glared at him.

Rosie sighed. After everything that happened, she was in denial for the first time. They were left with no murder weapon, no suspects, and no murderer. Along with the issue of *two* dead bodies.

After hesitating for a moment, she took a deep breath and began talking, her heart heavy at each word she said.

'So ... he just died?' Kyra whispered in shock once Rosie had finished.

'He was poisoned,' Rosie said, 'I'm sure of it.' She *was* sure of it, and just as sure that there was no way of confirming it.

'You can't prove it, though. No one would believe you.' Luca pointed out.

Rosie nodded in defeat. 'I know,' she muttered.

She remembered how pale Roberto's skin was, and how much his hands shook, as well as the fact that he had told her he had drunk whatever substance had been in that bottle.

'What do we do now?' Kyra asked. 'We have two dead bodies with two different murderers. And currently no suspects *or* motive.'

A long silence filled the room, broken by the scratching of the rose bush against the window, occasional crunching, and the sounds of people chatting around outside.

'Is it possible to track down Lazarus?'

At Luca's words, Razario croaked and squealed, chanting 'Lazarus' over and over.

Rosie glared at him. 'I doubt it. We know nothing about him. Aside from his name being Roberto's last words.'

Luca frowned. 'These murders aren't a coincidence. There must be something that links them together.'

'Revenge?' Kyra suggested. 'Perhaps Roberto's murderer didn't want Nico to die.'

'That can't be right.' Rosie shook her head.

'Roberto had the poison with him. He drank it willingly.'

'Maybe he didn't know it was poisoned.'

Rosie frowned. 'It's possible.'

She fell into silence again.

'We should treat this like a new investigation,' Kyra said after a pause. 'Find out who Roberto was, and anyone who could have known him. We may learn about Lazarus along the way.'

Rosie looked up. There weren't many other options, apart

from empty speculations, and aimless theories.

Kyra pulled out a notebook and pencil. 'Can you describe what Roberto looked like?'

Rosie smiled and nodded, sitting back in her chair. The image of Roberto's face flew into her mind. Though it had been dark, she could clearly remember the paper-thin scar on his lip, and that one of his eyes had been a darker shade of brown than the other.

Although they didn't know where to go from there, Rosie felt the same thrill she had when she had started the investigation.

Maybe it wasn't impossible after all.

XVIII

CREEPING FOOTSTEPS

Hours had passed and the three children still sat in the kitchen. The table was now crowded with stray papers and blunted pencils, an occasional empty bowl and a magnifying glass that reflected against the light from a single burning candle.

Kyra had gone through over six sheets of paper, trying to get a perfect replica of Roberto. Her fingers were covered with smudged graphite, her brow furrowed, her mouth pressed into a thin line.

'Are you *quite* finished?' Rosie demanded with impatience.

'Almost,' Kyra answered, rubbing the paper with the tip of her graphite covered thumb. After a few moments, she nodded to herself and held the paper out with a proud grin.

They marvelled at how she had captured each stray strand of hair, each crease beside the eyes.

Rosie beamed as Kyra handed her the sheet to look at. Luca peered over at it from behind Rosie's shoulder and gave a small grin, taking it from her hands to inspect it closer. Eventually, he handed it back to Kyra with a small, 'it's wonderful.'

Kyra grinned, and Rosie was almost surprised to see her

two front teeth overlapping. She wasn't sure why, but the idea of Kyra having such a tiny flaw was almost unbelievable; everything she did seemed to radiate perfection. It made her feel an odd sense of relief, as if she had been hoping for her to have a small imperfection, so she could be reminded that they were somewhat similar.

'But ... what do we do with this?' Luca gestured to the paper. 'We can't just go around asking strangers if they've seen a random man before.'

There was a small clutter from the table and everyone turned their heads. Razario had picked up the magnifying glass and brought it close to him, so that a large beaded eye shone through the lens. He leaned forward and pressed his face closer to Luca, who backed away slightly.

'He's a genius,' Razario croaked, moving the magnifying glass to and from his eye, as if examining Luca's expressions.

Rosie failed to hide her grin when Luca's eyes widened and his jaw dropped open.

'That's how he shows affection,' she muttered, trying to mask her laugh.

'It isn't,' Razario croaked, placing the magnifying glass down.

Rosie ignored him. 'It means he likes you.'

'It doesn't.'

Kyra chuckled and began rinsing the graphite from her fingertips. She paused as she reached over to dry her hands on a rag.

She bent to pick up one of Razario's tail feathers that had drifted onto the floor.

'Don't grey parrots have red tails?' she asked.

Rosie frowned. 'They do.'

'Then why is his one *blue*?'

Rosie looked up to the feather in Kyra's hand. From where she sat, it didn't look any different to how it always did.

'It's probably the light,' she muttered, brushing it off.

Kyra bit her lip, holding it up to the window and squinting.

'What colour is your tail, Razario?'

'It changes,' he croaked back.

Rosie chuckled. 'It doesn't.'

She glanced over at Luca, who shrugged and cleared his throat.

'We have a murder to solve, don't we?' he joked.

Kyra sighed. 'I suppose. I think I'll ask Gwydion if he knows anything.' She paused for a moment. 'If he'll even listen to a word I say.'

She had a bitter expression across her face, as if the idea of talking to her own brother was like drinking lemon juice.

Rosie frowned. 'You don't get on?'

Kyra looked down at her hands, chewing on her lip.

'We don't,' she said coldly. 'He's always away, and when he's back he makes little effort in showing his excitement to see us. He was probably waiting to leave, and coming back is just a bitter chore for him.'

Rosie wasn't sure what to say. From meeting Gwydion, she suspected he was a shy, awkward young man who cared too much about what others thought of him.

She supposed Kyra resented him for leaving her with her father. She knew they didn't get on particularly well.

'How long has he been travelling?' Luca asked.

'Three years. He managed to conveniently find a job right after mother died.'

Rosie frowned. 'He didn't stay to help?'

Kyra scoffed. She threw the rag onto the table with such force that the candlestick toppled over, wax spilling onto the wood. Luca was quick to jump up and snuff out the flame before chaos ensued, but Kyra's temper was still burning furiously.

'Nice work,' Razario teased, although his tone was almost approving, as if he agreed with her sudden outburst. Kyra glared at him.

'Of course he didn't stay to help,' she said, dropping into a seat and crossing her arms. 'Although I don't particularly blame him for leaving. Father was in such a state, I thought of running away too.' She chuckled a little, then dropped her gaze and cleared her throat.

'You should have,' Razario croaked.

She looked up at him with narrowed eyes and drew a breath. After a moment, however, she sighed and nodded.

'Maybe,' she muttered.

Rosie and Luca shared a glance. Neither of them knew how to reply.

Kyra stood and smoothed down her skirt.

'I'm leaving,' she said briskly, brushing her hair back.

'If Gwydion won't talk to me, I'm sure Alvar will know something.'

Luca frowned. 'You really think *Il Signore di Venezia* will give you his time?'

Kyra shrugged. 'He has before. What's the worst that could happen?'

'He'll kill you,' Razario offered simply.

Kyra did not reply, but instead fixed him with a pointed gaze.

Rosie cleared her throat. 'Nico's brother may also know something,' she said. She stood, but her movements were stopped by Kyra's curt voice.

'Where *do* you think you're going?' she demanded

pointedly, hands on hips.

'You can't leave the house, remember?'

Rosie swore, but did not sit back down. 'But I can't just sit here and wait!' she argued.

'You have to,' Luca persisted, gently shoving on her shoulder to get her to sit back down. 'Everyone has most likely seen the paper; they'll know what you look like. I don't fancy having to explain to my father why you're back at the police station again.'

Rosie glanced at him. He looked at her for a moment, then dropped his gaze and gave her an awkward smile.

Rosie crossed her arms and looked at Kyra, her eyebrows creased. Kyra mirrored Rosie's position, folding one arm over the other and tapping her foot, tilting her head to the side.

'Yes,' Razario squealed teasingly. 'Sit here and wait.'

'*Fine*,' Rosie agreed at last, glaring at the parrot with narrowed eyes.

'I'll stay.'

Kyra nodded. She opened up her satchel and chucked something to Rosie, who caught it neatly and looked down. It was Nico's notebook, she realised, a grin spreading across her face. She traced over the small star in the corner, her fingertips grazing the burnt leather.

'I brought it from your room,' Kyra said, 'thought you might find it useful.'

Rosie nodded, and Kyra moved over to the door. She looked over and Luca studied him for a moment.

'Are you coming?' she asked. He looked up, eyebrows raised.

'Erm ...' He hesitated, glancing back at Rosie.

'Go on,' she said, crossing her legs and leaning back in her chair. 'I'm not stopping you.'

He stood up, grabbed his coat from the back of his chair and threw it over his shoulders, waving a quick goodbye as he left.

Rosie watched him walk out of the house with an annoyed frown.

SLOWLY AND HEAVILY, time drawled by.

Rosie had spent the hours trying to understand what the contents of Nico's notebook meant; the letters jumbled up into strange-looking sentences, the rings of numbers surrounding odd symbols, the recurring sketch of the coin, that seemed to be on every other page.

She had stared at the paper for so long, the words and images were imprinted behind her eyes.

But she was still none the wiser.

Frowning, she ruffled absentmindedly through the dry pages until a hoot from Razario shifted her focus, and she looked up towards his perch.

'What?' she snapped. She was expecting him to answer, make a joke about how little she was helping, but instead, he stayed silent, blinking and inclining his head towards the window.

Sighing, Rosie turned her head back to the notebook, her eyes glazing over the jumbled letters, her leg tapping up and down restlessly.

Minutes felt like hours as she waited in the kitchen, her fingers tracing back and forth over the writing, pieces of scrap paper with written and rewritten words littered across the table. Her grandfather had taught her many codes when she was a child, and she had tried all of them, but none had worked.

She tutted and walked over to the window, pulling back

the curtain slightly so she could see outside, carefully, to keep her face hidden.

It was raining, the window pane covered in small droplets of water, chasing each other down the glass. The canal was rippling from the downpour, the gondolas parked neatly at the edge of the walkway.

Rosie closed the curtain slowly and turned back to the table. Taking the notebook and letting Razario perch on her arm, she trudged upstairs.

She was itching to be outside.

She wondered if Luca and Kyra had found any useful amount of information about the murder.

Perhaps they have already figured it out, Rosie thought, her eyebrows twisting together. More than anything, Rosie loved being outside. Even in the coldest winter days, she would spend hours walking by the canal. Now, with the risk of being arrested, she couldn't step foot out the door.

Rosie sighed and dropped down on the bed, closing her eyes and pinching the bridge of her nose in frustration. She wasn't sure she'd ever felt this useless before.

'You're *really* helping,' Razario mocked from his spot on the windowsill. Rosie's eyes snapped open.

'It's not as if I have anything better to do,' she shot back.

He let out a quiet sigh, looking over at her and flapping his wings, letting out various croaks to get her attention. She ignored him and he glared at her with beady eyes, then went back to biting feathers from his wings.

Rosie was lulled into sleep by the sound of raindrops pattering against the window, and was soon encased in the reality of looming silhouettes, vivid colours and overwhelming sounds.

She was soon woken, however, by a small thud from

downstairs, and the sound of light footsteps.

She frowned. Luca and Kyra shouldn't be back so soon. From the windowsill, Razario had stopped ruffling his feathers and was now leaning closer to the door.

Rosie moved off the bed, wincing each time the floorboards creaked underneath her. Her hand made contact with the door, and she pulled it open, so that it was easier for her to identify the sounds.

They were definitely footsteps, but not the heavy, confident ones that she had heard from Luca; they were quiet – hesitant.

Rosie looked back at Razario with wide eyes and he tilted his head back and forth, as if shaking it in protest of her actions.

She could have sworn he whispered the word 'Lazarus' under his breath, but when she turned to him, he was silent.

She must have imagined it. She hadn't been able to shake off the name since Roberto had uttered it that night; she had heard it in her dreams, whispered over and over like an endless echo.

Rosie closed the door and tiptoed down the hallway, taking short, quiet breaths.

Everything was still.

Until she heard it.

Another set of breathing.

The hairs on the back of her neck stood on end, as the feeling of cold air puffed against her skin.

She froze. She almost couldn't turn around. She squeezed her eyes shut, willing everything to stop, or for it all to have been a bad dream.

But the breathing was still there, steady against her neck.

Rosie turned, her movements stiff.

He was dressed all in black, and his face was covered by a

dark cloth. Only his eyes were showing, and a paper-thin scar ran over one of them, bumpy against his skin.

Rosie wanted to scream, but his hand flew to her mouth. She wanted to struggle, but he was far too strong.

Their faces were so close together, she could see her fear reflected in his dusky eyes, and smell the cigarettes from his breath.

The man took a step back, and before Rosie could comprehend what was happening, something heavy hit the side of her head, and the world faded away.

XIX

UNWANTED COMPANY

LUCA FOLLOWED close beside Kyra, as she led him into a secluded part of Venice. The roads twisted and the corridors tightened, alleyways darkened and paths transformed from smooth walkways to jagged rocks, stabbing dully at their feet as they strode past. Buildings were crooked silhouettes against a carpet of dark grey. Lampposts were half hidden by clouds of thick mist, which loomed over the city like an unreliable dream. Glowing lanterns cast soft shadows on the slick roads as people dashed past. Rain soaked the rags that were laid out to dry, or thundered through half open windows.

Kyra fiddled with her dress and tutted over her scuffed shoes, as they approached a large building. It looked old and torn-down; wooden panels rattled loosely in the breeze, window panes were covered in spider web cracks and the stone steps leading to the rotten door were chipped and dirty.

'*Il Signore di Venezia* lives here?' Luca asked in disbelief. He had heard of this man before, of the control he held over Venice, how he tainted conversations with his bloodstained name. He suspected someone who called himself 'The Lord

Of Venice' would live like royalty.

Kyra nodded. 'He does. Don't let the exterior fool you. And remember that he's a dangerous man, so don't say anything to anger him.' She glanced at him and reached up to fix his collar, eyebrows furrowed.

'In fact, don't say anything at all. Just let me do the talking.'

Luca shrugged and nodded. Kyra took a slow breath, then lifted a gloved hand to the door and knocked twice. She took a step back and brushed her hair behind her shoulders, clearing her throat. Not long after, the door opened, and the familiar face of the old butler peeked through. He let out an audible sigh and swung the door closed, though Kyra's hand was already blocking it from clicking shut.

'It's terribly important and we'll only be a few minutes,' she said.

The old man snarled. 'I find it hard to believe you aren't at the bottom of the Grand Canal,' he sighed, as he opened the door.

'You're lucky he has patience for you.'

He stepped aside and the two children walked through. Luca's eyes instantly widened. The room was large, and the walls were covered in heavily gilded paper. Mahogany furniture sat heavily in the centre of the room, large, polished chairs surrounding a long, sturdy table which was covered in a thick cloth.

There was a door in the far end of the room, and faint music could be heard from behind it.

'Wait here,' the butler said. 'Do not move and do not touch *anything*.' At that, he looked directly to Luca, who glared at him and pressed his lips together.

He disappeared behind the door, leaving the two of them alone. Luca reached over to examine a large vase, but was stopped when Kyra grabbed his wrist.

'*Don't*,' she hissed. 'If Alvar decides he doesn't like us, he *will* kill us. You have a father, remember? What will he do when he finds out his son has been murdered for disobeying the most powerful man in Venice?'

Luca huffed. 'Fine,' he grumbled, pulling his hand back.

The door on the far side of the room opened again, and the butler strode through.

'He will see you now,' he said, bitterness in his voice.

He led them into a darkened corridor, walls laden with portraits in gilded frames. He opened another door, and ushered them through, then shut it with a scowl.

A man sat on a large red armchair, a thick cigar in between his fingers. He grinned at them, and a gold tooth glistened against the light.

'Wonderful to see you again, Kyra,' he said.

Kyra stiffened. 'I never told you my name,' she muttered.

He shrugged off her comment. 'You never had to. I make a point to learn about everyone who visits me, and after a small amount of research, I know you. I know your family and your friends, I know everything about you.'

He glanced over at Luca, eyes narrowing. 'You, however, I do not know.'

Luca cleared his throat. 'I'm helping Rosie,' he said.

Alvar smirked. 'I see. Take a seat.'

He gestured to the large sofa opposite him and the two of them gingerly sat down.

'How can I be of service?' His tone was light when he spoke, as if he were playing a game with a child.

Kyra pulled a sheet of paper from her satchel, covered with the drawing she had done of Roberto.

'Have you seen this man?'

He took the paper from her hands and studied it. His eyes shifted across the sheet, brow furrowed.

After a moment, he shook his head.

'He killed Nico?'

Kyra nodded. 'Then dropped dead before he could be taken in.'

Alvar looked as if he wanted to laugh. Instead, he took a long puff of his cigar and handed the paper back.

'I'm afraid there's nothing I can do to help.'

Kyra frowned. She folded the paper and stuck into her notebook.

'He mentioned the name 'Lazarus' before he died. Have you heard it before?' she asked.

Alvar paused. He pushed the end of his cigar into a copper ashtray until a thin trail of smoke rose into the air.

'I don't believe the name has come up,' he said, walking over to the far side of the room with hands clasped behind his back.

Luca and Kyra shared confused glances.

Alvar reached over to his desk and picked up the newspaper, rifling through.

'It seems your friend is in a lot of trouble with the police,' he muttered with an almost-chuckle.

Kyra didn't know how to answer. 'It wasn't her fault,' she said at last.

Alvar shook his head. 'I suppose not. She ought to have been more cautious.'

Luca wasn't sure why he felt the urge to defend her. He opened his mouth to speak, but was cut off when Kyra gently elbowed him. He pressed his lips together and crossed his arms.

Alvar tossed the paper down and opened the door to his office.

'That will be all, I think,' he said, gesturing to the exit. 'See yourselves out.'

LUCA PUSHED through the crowds in a hurry, his hand held above his head to protect himself from the rain. It didn't work, as his hair was now sticking to his face, and his clothes were soaked through.

He and Kyra had parted ways when she had decided to visit her brother. She had given Luca a small scrap of paper with an address scrawled on his messy letters.

He arrived at the address after half an hour of walking, and knocked on the door, blinking into the rain as he waited.

The door opened after a few moments, and a woman looked out. She had watery brown eyes and a weary smile.

'May I help you?'

After a brief explanation of why he was there, Luca smiled and brought out the paper from his coat pocket. It was slightly damp and wilted, but the picture Kyra had drawn was still clear.

'Do you recognize this man?'

The woman thought for a moment, then shook her head. She took the picture from his hands and called into the house. A moment later, a man walked through.

He had looked tired and worn out, as if he hadn't slept in days. He looked at the photo, but shook his head almost instantly, handing the page back.

'Never seen him,' he muttered, 'did he kill my brother?'

Luca hesitated, but gave a slow nod.

'So it wasn't that girl then.' It wasn't a question, but it almost wanted to be one.

Luca shook his head. 'It wasn't her.'

The man nodded, then gave a half-smile and shut the door.

Luca frowned, but turned away and hurried back to his

house, blinking through the haze of rain

He hadn't been travelling for long before he'd noticed someone following him. He continued calmly, picking up his pace as he made his way home. His stalker began to walk faster, and when Luca glanced into a puddle, the glint of a knife caught his eye.

He turned into an empty alleyway and ran, glancing behind him to check if he was still being followed. He was. The man walked behind him swiftly, concealing the knife he held in between the fold of his thick coat.

Luca was beginning to panic; he turned quickly into another alley, his feet skimming across the slippery cobbles. He looked up and swore under his breath. The alleyway ended with a large brick wall, its stone structure looming over him as he stood, frozen in place. The man behind him had caught up and was now only metres away, walking over with determined footsteps.

Luca turned, desperate to keep his composure.

'Who are you?' He demanded.

The man didn't reply. He didn't need to, for Luca already knew this was about Roberto's death.

He stepped forward, taking a slow breath.

The man walked closer, wordlessly drawing out the knife from his coat.

Luca shifted his feet to the side.

He knew how to protect himself; hours training in his father's stadium had given him much practice. But he had never been in a real fight before, and this man had a weapon, one that he meant to do harm with.

The man lunged forward, holding the blade in his outstretched hand. Luca stepped neatly to the side and grabbed the man's wrist, pulling it down and twisting harshly, so that he stumbled and dropped to the floor.

Luca kicked the knife that had clattered to the ground, sending it skittering across the stone.

He smirked and tugged at the man's arm, making him grunt in annoyance.

'What do you want with me?!' Luca demanded.

The man didn't answer.

Luca twisted the man's arm sharply, and he cried out in pain.

'It's about the girl. They're coming for her.'

In a flash, Luca had let go of the man's arm, risen quickly, and dashed down the alley. He skidded and faltered, as if his feet couldn't quite catch up with him. But none of that mattered; he had to make sure Rosie was still safe. As he approached his house, he flung open the door and stumbled inside.

'Rosie?' he yelled, kicking off his shoes. 'Where are you?'

No answer. He ran upstairs and threw open the bedroom door. Only Razario was inside, tapping his beak repeatedly against the window pane.

'Where is she?' Luca was breathless.

'Took her,' Razario croaked.

'Who took her?'

'The man,' Razario replied, flying over to where Luca stood. Luca groaned and ran a hand through his hair.

'We have to find her,' he said, 'she's in danger.'

'Really?' Razario mocked. 'Pretty boy *must* save her.'

There were a few moments of silence, in which Luca steadied his breathing and headed back downstairs.

'Stay here,' he told Razario, 'and tell father what happened.'

Razario answered only by flapping his wings too close to Luca's face, catching his hair with his claws. Luca glared at him and Razario let out a croaky chuckle.

Before Luca could leave the house, a thud sounded from the

ground below. He frowned and walked over to the basement door, swinging it open.

It was dark, and there was a layer of water on the stone floor. Leaving the door open for light, he crept down the stairs, the cold stone dulling his steps as he descended.

A faint splash sounded from behind him, and the door swung closed, blocking all but a sliver of light from entering the room.

Luca whipped his head round. A dark shadow flickered across the wall, but it was gone before he could blink.

It was then that he saw the silhouette, stapled against the door.

Luca's heartbeats were footsteps, coming closer and closer towards him, as he stood, frozen, in the almost-darkness.

There was a man in the room.

He was standing perfectly still, hands clasped behind his back, almost as if he was waiting.

Luca turned on his heels, pushing his hands upwards. But the man had shifted positions, and Luca's hand met with nothing but thin air. The man clasped an arm around Luca's neck in one swift movement.

Luca gasped for breath, tugging at the man's hold in a futile attempt to wrench his arm away.

It didn't work.

Luca's head began to spin, and black dots appeared before his eyes. He tried to blink them away, but to no avail.

The man's grip grew tighter, and Luca could feel his world slowly fading away.

Fading...

    Fading...

        Fading.

XX

A BREWING STORM

The rain thundered against the cobbles, splashing on Kyra's dress as she pushed hurriedly through gathered crowds. After leaving Luca to speak with Alfie and Irene, she was headed to see her brother.

She wasn't sure Gwydion would know anything about Roberto; he was never the type who paid close attention to details, and he would often stay away from people, not wishing to get too involved in affairs that were none of his business.

She chewed on her bottom lip as she walked. The hem of her dress was now soaked with dirty water, and her gloved hands were clenched into tight fists.

She was still finding it hard to believe the situation she was in; investigating a crime while one of her very few friends was being held accountable for a murder she hadn't committed. She wondered if her father had noticed her disappearance. Maybe he just didn't care. Kyra had considered telling him about the murders, but she knew what his reaction would be; an angry lecture about the danger she was getting herself into, followed by the order to stay in her room until she had 'come to her senses.'

But although solving a murder was was far beyond anything Kyra had ever done, it wasn't as difficult as she had thought it would be. She had always been drawn to puzzles and mystery, and would often spend hours reading stories, not unlike her current situation, snuggled in bed, under the soft glow of candlelight.

Her life before meeting Rosie was particularly uninteresting, stuck alone all day with nothing but books and music. Occasionally, someone important and educated would come to talk business with her father, often bringing an elegant, well spoken daughter, or a son, who was only there to make his parents look better.

Kyra had been forced into countless futile conversations, dressed up for fancy evenings with older men of whom she knew nothing about, and presented at parties as the frail daughter of a rich businessman, one that caused no trouble, did what she was told, and stuck to the orders of her father, an obedient, well-behaved child, with no thoughts or desires of her own.

How wrong they were.

Kyra did have thoughts and desires, she had a mind, as well as beauty; she had talent, as well as charm. She wasn't an object people stared at or admired; she was a person, and her family didn't see it. Even her brother, whom Kyra had tried to convince otherwise, was fixated on the idea that all young ladies should be well-spoken and listen to the orders of older men.

But somehow, after less than a day of knowing her, Rosie had seen otherwise.

Rosie must understand what it feels like, Kyra thought, as she slowly approached her house. *Perhaps there are others who are angry with society's unrealistic demands.*

Kyra looked up, snapping out of her thoughts as her gloved hand met the green paint of her wooden door. After a few moments, the sound of approaching footsteps could be heard, and the door swung open.

Gwydion looked down at her with concern. He barely waited for her to step inside before wrapping his arms around her.

'We've looked everywhere for you,' he murmured, as he pulled away and hung up her coat.

'Father was ready to ask the police.'

'I've only been gone a day,' Kyra muttered with annoyance as she followed him inside.

'You're not allowed to leave the house, Kyra! We discussed this!'

Gwydion moved over to the stairs, but Kyra stopped him from going up.

'Don't call him; I'm leaving in a minute.'

Gwydion gave her a look that was almost amusement. Almost, but not quite.

'You're not leaving,' he muttered, grabbing her arm. Kyra shook herself from his grip and glared at him.

'I really don't think you have any choice in my whereabouts; *you're* never even here.'

Gwydion frowned deeply. 'What *has* gotten into you? You never disobey.'

'I've decided that I don't agree with father's decision to keep me locked up. I'm capable of handling myself.'

Gwydion sighed and pinched the bridge of his nose.

'I ought to call him down. You know he won't allow this.'

'I really don't care, Gwydion. I'm only here to ask you if you've seen this man.'

Kyra pulled open her satchel and drew out a picture. It was

a rough of the one she had drawn earlier, but it held the most important details: the small, paper-thin scar that trailed over his lip, the right eye slightly darker than the other. She had passed the original to Luca earlier in the day.

Gwydion frowned as his eyes grazed over the page, then shook his head in defeat.

'I've never seen him before.'

Kyra nodded, already knowing where she was to go next. Before she could reach the door, however, Gwydion grabbed her arm.

'What are you doing, Kyra? Please don't tell me you're helping that little detective girl ...'

Kyra bristled, pulling her arm away. 'Maybe I am,' she muttered. 'What would it matter to you?'

'Kyra ...' Gwydion sighed and pinched the bridge of his nose. 'You're a pretty young lady, you have a rich father, and you were brought up in an educated environment. You have so many great options for your life; why are you choosing to investigate *murders?* Surely there's something more ... appropriate that you can do.'

'I won't sit around here and let you and father treat me as if I'm incapable and docile.' Krya paused. She had been meaning to say how she really felt for a while, but every time she opened her mouth, the words had died out before they even reached the tip of her tongue.

'I'm tired of being locked away, forcing myself into tight dresses and attending events that don't interest me.'

Kyra looked up, locking gazes with her brother. He seemed almost apologetic, like there was something he could have done to help her.

'I understand, but you have no other choice—'

'Yes, I do! I do have a choice, you just don't agree with it.'

Gwydion furrowed his brow, choosing his next words carefully.

'This is dangerous,' he said at last, speaking in a low voice, 'and you could get seriously hurt, or worse!'

'I'm aware of the risks!' Kyra yelled, throwing open the door, the cold wind beating against her face, 'and I know what I'm doing.'

Then, without another word, Kyra stepped out into the rain, slamming the door in her brother's face.

XXI

SHATTERED REALITIES

Darkness.
Rosie awoke groggily.

She was lying on the ground. The room around her was shaded, and the floor beneath her head was hard and cold.

She flexed her hands. They were tied tightly behind her back, causing her wrists to ache and itch.

Her memory was foggy, and she could only recall a few details of the events that had brought her here – the man in black, a scarred eye, the feeling of something cold and heavy hitting her head.

She squeezed her eyes shut, trying to focus. The air was heavy with the scent of salt and seaweed, and the floorboards beneath her were rocking.

She was on a boat.

She opened her eyes and blinked into the darkness.

Features and shapes began to emerge before her, lit up by a thin sliver of light that snaked through the crack in the ceiling; a ladder, leading up to a hatch above her head, and the soft silhouettes of large, looming crates.

Rosie's heart hammered against her chest; her head was

aching. She drew a deep breath and felt around behind her for something sharp to cut her ropes, which were digging painfully into her skin.

Her hands trailed over the floor, until they caught on a cold glass bottle. She considered smashing it against the floor, but quickly stopped herself; it was likely that she wasn't alone, and she didn't want her captors to hear her trying to escape.

She sighed and scraped her palms against the walls of the boat, feeling around for a spike instead. Her hands grabbed aimlessly at the wall, but she was unsuccessful in her search. Rosie sighed and stood up, placing her eyes against the crack in the planks. She squinted for a better view, but could only see a thin line of light grey above her.

She tried to lean forward, but was interrupted by the sound of heavy footsteps coming towards her.

She sat back down against the floor, bringing her knees to her chest.

The hatch above her opened and a burst of light revealed two men coming down the stairs: one tall and muscular, with a large tattoo of a snake spiralling up his arm; the other shorter and far less robust, a grimace plastered across his face, his eyes squinting to adjust to the darkness. There was someone behind them, Rosie realised, and she moved her head to get a better look. Though her view was blocked by one of the men, a wave of relief washed over her, and she smiled.

'Luca?'

The boy looked up. In the half-light, Rosie could make out a small cut across his bottom lip. His eyes brightened, and he gave her a small grin before he was shoved roughly down the creaking stairs.

'Don't move,' the tattooed man grunted and closed the hatch back up again, leaving Rosie and Luca in the dark.

'Are you alright?' Luca asked the moment the footsteps died away. His hands were also latched tightly behind him, and he tugged at them in annoyance.

Rosie nodded and looked up. 'We have to get out of here,' she whispered. She pulled at her wrists, but the rope didn't loosen, and instead became painfully tight. She groaned and sat down on the steps.

'Where are we?' she asked after a moment's pause.

'They're taking us to an island,' Luca said. 'I suppose we were beginning to get in their way.'

Rosie hesitated. 'They could have just killed us,' she muttered.

Luca chuckled. 'Don't sound so disappointed. We must have been getting close to something if they decided to take us out of the picture.'

'If only we knew what that was,' Rosie groaned. Then, 'Did you find out anything from the other suspects?'

Luca shook his head. '*Il Signore di Venezia* didn't give us any new clues, and I talked to Nico's brother, but he didn't know anything. Kyra was going to talk to her brother when I saw her last.'

'I hope she's okay,' Rosie muttered.

She wondered what Kyra was doing now, or if she had discovered anything new.

*Maybe she's in even more dang*er, she thought with a shiver. From what she had gathered, Kyra wasn't the best at protecting herself, and without Rosie or Luca, she could be in serious danger.

Luca frowned. 'Are you certain you're alright?' he asked, glancing at her with worried eyes.

'I'm not sure.' She closed her eyes. All she could picture was a terrified Kyra, being backed into an alleyway by someone holding a long, sharp knife. She winced.

'What should we do?' Luca's question drew Rosie from her thoughts with a snap.

Luca opened his mouth to speak, but was interrupted by the hatch flying open and the two men standing outside.

'Get out,' the tattooed one grunted, grabbing Rosie's arm and forcing her up the stairs. She blinked, the cold air slapping her face, the grip on her arm tightening when she tried to move. It was still daytime, and the sky was plastered with grey clouds, raindrops pattering against the deck of the boat, which was moored up by a bank of grass, the mooring rope attached to a long piece of wood that jutted out of the water at an crooked angle .

The taller man shoved Rosie to the end of the boat with a loud grunt, and she stepped off, Luca following her with a scowl.

Rosie realised what they were doing now, as she stepped onto the soggy grass. They were going to leave them on the island and get away with murder. She shot a worried glance at Luca, whose eyebrows were knotted together, and knew he had come to the same conclusion.

Once Rosie and Luca were on the grass, the taller man undid the mooring rope and began winding it up.

'You can't just leave us here!' Rosie tried. She was greeted with nothing but a chuckle.

'We have no reason not to. You're in our way.' The man spoke curtly, as if saying any more syllables would use all his energy. He smirked, and as his foot kicked off the grass, the boat drifted away from the island, leaving Rosie and Luca standing on the mop of wet grass, watching as it bobbed off, until it was nothing more than a spot in the distance. Rosie sighed and turned her head to look at the island. They weren't too far from the mainland; Rosie could still see the soft outline of the city through the haze of rain.

'We need to get out of here,' she mumbled, glancing around her. They were surrounded by a gathering of tall trees, their leaves sagging with the weight of the water, small droplets of dew spilling down their waxy surface like blood from torn skin.

'That's not going to happen,' Luca muttered. 'We don't have a boat or raft, and there's no way we'd be able to swim back from here.'

Rosie glared at him and dropped down to sit on a stone. 'You're right,' she said, her voice dull. Her hands met with the cold stone and a smile formed across her face. Rosie bent down and scrambled through the grasses, letting out a satisfied exclamation as she picked up a sharp piece of flint.

'Help me cut through the rope,' she muttered, handing Luca the stone.

The next few minutes were filled with annoyed exclamations and many attempts to cut through the rope, until the two parts fell limply to the grass. Rosie rubbed her wrists with a grin and began to untie Luca's ropes. Luca beamed, turning to face her. Rosie tried to ignore how he was only inches away from her, and how she seemed to lose sense of time when she stared into his eyes. She stood and walked to the grass.

'We should look around,' she muttered, hitching up her skirt as she trudged through the wet. The long grass reached the top of her boots, scratching her legs as she pulled her skirt up. The mud beneath her was soft, and if she lingered in it for too long, she seemed to sink into it.

Luca shrugged and followed behind her, stepping with care in the spots between the grass and mud.

Rosie kept her eyes on the ground as she walked, her mind

drifting away, far from where it should be, to a memory of her grandfather's voice, rough like sandpaper.

'*Keep calm, and use your surroundings to benefit yourself.*'

Rosie took a deep breath and stepped forward. She stopped, as her shoes made contact with a hard plank. It seemed to crack under her feet, and she looked up quickly, fixing her gaze on Luca as it crumbled underneath her. Just like that, she fell, screaming as her body plummeted into a hole. She hit the ground hard and looked up, wincing as a stone dug into her palm, a thin line of blood trickling down her hand. Luca was by the edge of the hole in seconds, peering down with worry in his eyes.

'Are you alright?' he called, his voice echoing down the gap.

Rosie nodded, glancing around. It was dark, but Rosie's eyes caught a small glow coming from somewhere not so far ahead.

'Can you come down here?'

Luca nodded and jumped down, landing softly on his feet, one hand resting on the ground. Rosie stared at him for possibly a moment too long, for when he looked up, he caught her eye, then tilted his head to the side with an amused smirk.

Rosie averted her stare and looked to the side.

The indistinct blur of a light that seemed too close and too far away had caught her eye.

She nudged Luca, but he was staring down at her hand.

'You're bleeding,' he said.

'It doesn't matter. Look.'

She pointed ahead, and Luca followed her gaze to the light. He frowned and walked closer to the end of the pit, disappearing round the corner. Rosie heard his exclamation of excitement and chased after him.

The cave didn't end where she thought it would; instead,

a staircase was carved into the stone. The steps were wide and shallow, and they spiralled down the side of the cave. The crumbling walls to the left of the staircase were covered in a strange sort of algae. That was what seemed to be giving off the light. It was almost vibrating off the walls. There was nothing to the right of the stairs except a steep drop into what Rosie presumed were another level of caves.

She looked around her in an almost dazed state of shock. Ahead of her, Luca was trailing his hands along the wall of the cave, eyes wide.

The steps were slippery and glistening with the hazy reflection of the bright green light that radiated off the cavern's walls. Every step she took echoed into the seemingly bottomless cavern, the sound echoing hollowly off the walls. She followed Luca wordlessly down the stairs, treading carefully, using the uneven wall to her left to guide her down.

They walked down in silence, too focused on making sure they didn't fall.

But that silence was broken when the stone underneath Rosie's foot crumbled away.

A loud shriek left her lips, as her foot slipped off the stone. She grasped at the wall, and Luca grabbed at her arm to stop her from falling off the stairs completely.

She took a deep breath and looked at him as she regained her balance. He gave her a worried smile, and refused to let go of her wrist until there were no more stairs left to walk down.

It was dark at the bottom of the steps, and with only the glow of the fluorescent substance on the walls, every shape was a lurking silhouette. Stalactites loomed threateningly above them, jagged rocks menaced from the shadows, and hollow caverns were empty beckoning voids of blackness. Beside her, Luca's eyes darted around the cave, his hands in nervous fists.

There was a small chamber on the far side of the cavern, and Rosie moved closer. Hesitantly.

Inside the entrance, strange objects and coins spilled from rotting boxes, and a large crystal was perched on a stone column, which had strange carvings engraved on its sides.

She had never seen anything like it. The crystal's edges were ragged and bumpy, but the faces were almost perfectly smooth. It was large, resembling the shape of a tooth, with long sides with a pointed cap.

Rosie moved closer, running her hands along its surface. A small droplet of her blood fell onto the crystal, and she scrubbed at it hastily.

'Are you sure you should do that?' Luca asked from where he was standing, examining a chalice with jewels crusted along its edge. Rosie didn't answer; instead, she circled the stone, keeping her eyes fixed on the colour in the middle. It was mesmerising, and she had to force herself to stop looking at it.

'Where *are* we?' she mumbled, half to herself. She looked down at her feet and found small shining jewels crunching under her shoes. She bent down and picked one up. It was covered in the same algae that was on the tunnel wall, bright green light glaring out. Rosie rubbed the stone, and the algae coated her fingertips; it was soft and slimy, and she wiped it off quickly.

She had seen this before.

'Luca!' She called. He looked up from his spot on the floor.

'Something wrong?' he asked. Rosie shook her head. 'I think Nico was here,' she muttered, sniffing the algae to confirm her suspicion. She recognised the smell: cold, damp, and that unforgettable odour that made her head hurt.

'This algae was on one of his keys.' she said. 'Do you think he could have come down here before he died?'

Luca frowned. 'What would he be looking for down here?'

'I'm not sure,' she murmured, looking back at the crystal, the violet mist swirling inside. Rosie bent down and peered at the carvings in the stone. Her eyes glazed over a word, and she had to read it twice to make sure it was right.

It was.

Lightwing.

'*What?*' She traced her fingertips over the word. Luca looked up from where he was sitting, a small golden coin in his hand.

'Look,' Rosie whispered. He moved to sit beside her, his eyes widening as he read.

'Lightwing,' he murmured, 'but ...' he trailed off, looking at Rosie expectantly. She could only muster a half-hearted shrug. Luca bent down and picked something up from the ground.

'Does this look familiar to you?' he asked, holding it out to her.

In his palm, lay a small hexagonal coin. There was a crescent moon on the front, circling a small hole, and feathers engraved along its edge.

Rosie's eyes widened.

'It really wasn't the only one,' she muttered, her voice quiet. *Grandfather had lied to me.*

She took it from his hand, tracing her finger along the markings. The coin was warm in the palm of her hand.

'Why would Nico have come here?' She muttered. 'What could he possibly gain from all of this?'

Luca shrugged. Rosie dropped to her knees and began searching through the objects on the ground. Her hands grazed past a small, tear-shaped stone that seemed to change colour when she held it to the dim light.

As she stood up, a bright light emerged from the crystal, blanketing the cave in a sharp glow. She gasped and jumped backwards, grabbing Luca's arm, who took a hasty step away.

'What did you do?!' he demanded.

'Nothing! I wasn't even near it!'

The light got brighter and sharper, and Rosie was forced to close her eyes, dropping to her knees to bury her head from the glow.

A rippling shape emerged from the haze, and when Rosie looked up, they were no longer alone.

XXII

LIGHTWING

KYRA HESITATED at the entrance to the passageway. This part of Venice was unfamiliar to her. It was dark, cold. Shadows loomed, passageways tightened and narrowed, and at the far end of the street stood a single, broken-down house, a dim light seeping through the slits in the closed door.

Kyra took a deep breath, shivered, straightened her dress and walked forward, her shoes skidding on the broken step in front of the entrance. She reached up to knock on the door, but before her hand met with the wood, it swung open and bashed against the wall. Frowning, she stepped closer, shutting the door firmly behind her.

'Sofia?' she called, 'are you here?'

There was no reply, and the only answer Kyra received was from the crackling fire, and the dripping of water from somewhere not too far away. On the other side of the room, the door to the kitchen was ajar, revealing a warm glow from inside. Kyra pulled the door open further and stepped through.

The kitchen, like the rest of the house, was dirty and broken. The cupboards were old and splintered; the drawer pulled off its hinge. A slow dribble of water spluttered from the tap, and in the sink, the dishes were chipped and unwashed. The floorboards beneath Kyra's feet were stained and pulled apart, separating from each other, revealing a dusty surface underneath.

Kyra grimaced, pulling a spider's web from her hair.

A sudden gust of cold air hit her face and she looked up, noticing a small brick archway, the door open, leading outside. Stepping through, she found Sofia, leaning against a low brick wall, a glass of red wine in her hand.

She frowned at Kyra, shaking her head.

'Really? Will you two *ever* leave me alone?'

Kyra forced a pleasant smile on her face, standing straighter. 'Have you seen this man before?' she asked, pulling the slightly crumpled sheet of paper from her leather satchel. Sofia studied the paper, and for a moment, her eyes widened. Then, she shook her head and handed it back.

'No. I can't help you.' Her voice was dry, and she took a sip of wine with a sigh.

'You're lying,' said Kyra, waving the sheet of paper in front of her face. 'You have seen him before, haven't you?'

Sofia shook her head again. 'I don't know what you're talking about,' she muttered, closing her eyes.

Kyra ignored Sofia's reply.

'Was he at the Carnival?'

Sofia looked up. Her eyes hardened and she rolled her tongue over her teeth.

'Fine,' she breathed, throwing her hands in the air.

'He was at the Carnival.'

'What was he doing?' Kyra leant against the wall, grimacing at the layer of mud that coated the stone.

'He was talking to Nico ... I heard him mention someone

named Edward ... Does that help you?'

Kyra paused. Alvar had talked about Edward, but from what he had said, Kyra believed it would be almost impossible to find him.

She nodded. 'Did you hear anything else?' she asked. Sofia shook her head. 'Not enough to understand what was going on. I only caught the mention of Edward's name.' she said, taking another sip of wine and swallowing with a wince.

'I think you should go now, I don't have anything else to tell you.'

Kyra hesitated. She glanced over to the kitchen then back at Sofia, who was pulling herself up to sit on the wall, dangling her legs off the edge. After a moment's thought, Kyra nodded to herself, bade Sofia a pleasant goodbye, then left the building, walking back through the thin alleyway and into the busy courtyards.

THERE WAS A MAN in the cave.

He was tall, and his long white beard dragged onto the floor. His face was etched with the look of someone who has seen too many things.

The smile he wore did not reach his eyes.

A long white robe covered his hands, and had small pictures embroidered into its sleeves. It was almost glowing, although Rosie refused to believe it.

'Hello Rosie,' the old man said, opening his arms in welcome.

Luca stepped forward and put his arm in front of her. 'Who are you?' He demanded.

The old man offered a warm smile. 'My name is Axle. I'm here to help you both.'

There was a strange haze surrounding him, and it seemed

to vibrate as he spoke.

Rosie took a step closer, reaching out her hand. Part of her wanted him to be a figment of her imagination. That he was something she was making up, or that the algae had just tricked her into seeing things.

But as her fingertips brushed with his hand, she let out a small gasp and drew back.

He was cold. Almost as cold as Nico had been.

'How did you get here?' she demanded.

Axle shrugged. 'I've always been here. I've been waiting for you for a long time. I must say, I'm surprised. I expected Alfred to be with you.'

Rosie narrowed her eyes. 'How do you know my grandfather?'

'I know your entire family, Rosie. I knew your parents, grandparents, great-grandparents, and many more.'

Rosie scoffed. 'That's impossible. You're not hundreds of years old.'

Axle gave her a smile and offered a knowing look.

Rosie's eyes widened. 'This is a joke,' she muttered, looking over at Luca, who gave her a confused shrug.

'Do I look like I'm joking?' Axle's voice was clear.

'I would have expected you to know about me already. Alfred hasn't explained it all to you yet?'

Rosie hesitated. 'Yet?'

Axle nodded. 'If he hasn't told you by now, I suppose he must be waiting for the right time.'

'I haven't seen my grandfather in nearly three years,' Rosie said.

Axle's face changed. The light behind his eyes seemed to disappear, and his smile dropped to a tired frown.

'I see. Then perhaps my suspicions are correct.'

'What suspicions?' Rosie demanded.

'That your grandfather is lost to us forever.'

Rosie shook her head. 'You're wrong,' she said, although her voice came out more strained than she had wanted it to be.

'I hope I am,' Axle muttered.

A cold silence followed, pierced only by the dulled sound of water dripping from somewhere in the cave.

'What is this place?' Luca asked, after the only sound in the cave was the dripping water, and the soft *chink* of droplets against jewels.

'This is where the Lightwings left their discoveries,' Axle said.

Luca frowned, his grey eyes darkening slightly.

'Discoveries?'

Axle nodded. 'Some prefer to call it treasure, but I've always resented the word. It makes everything less ... magical.'

Rosie scoffed. 'Why would my family need *treasure*?'

Axle raised his eyebrows. 'You seem to know very little about pirates. As the daughter of two of them, I would have thought you'd understand.'

Rosie let out an unamused laugh. '*Pirates*?!'

Axle nodded. 'Don't look so surprised, Rosie. Your entire family comes from a line of them.'

Rosie looked to Luca, who seemed to be fighting the urge to laugh.

'Where did you expect all of these things to be from?' Axle asked, gesturing around the room.

Rosie gave him a look of pure disbelief.

She bent down and picked up a small piece of paper. Out of everything in the room, it seemed to be the only thing that wasn't made from a precious metal, and Rosie wondered how it had stayed intact.

She brushed it off with her thumb and stared down at the words written on it.

Rosie gasped, reading it over to make sure she hadn't imagined it. She hadn't.

In small, curling letters, a single word was written, and it seemed to imprint itself into Rosie's mind.

Lazarus.

XXIII

RESCUE

KYRA'S LEATHER SATCHEL swung by her sides, and her earrings bashed lightly against her neck.

Her heels slipped and stumbled, and the bottom of her dress was now weighed down with slippery mud.

After careful consideration, she had decided to see if there were any witnesses of Roberto's death. Unfortunately, she had been unsuccessful. She questioned three people, and they each gave her the same vague answer; that it had been far too dark to see anything that night, and they weren't particularly interested in the buildings when the festivities were in full play.

Kyra sighed. She was about to turn back when she felt someone lightly tap her shoulder.

An old lady was standing behind her, her face wrinkled, her hands trembling with age. She was wearing a dark dress, with sleeves that covered her fingers and a long skirt, trailing on the ground. She had a long, dark black cane in her hand, and she leant on it heavily.

'Excuse me, miss.' Kyra was surprised when she wasn't talking in Italian, but with a thick English accent instead. 'I heard you were asking about ... that night.' As she emphasised, *that night*, her eyes darted left and right, as if someone was listening to their conversation.

Kyra nodded, leading the women to a bench opposite the canal. 'Did you see anything strange?' she asked.

The old lady nodded. 'Yes, there was someone watching what happened from another building.'

She set down her cane and pointed to a rooftop in the distance. From where they were, it was only a dark shadow, looming against the mist. 'He didn't do anything,' the old lady said, her voice wavering. 'He simply ... stood there, staring at that troubled young lady.'

The old woman paused, moving her hand back to her cane, holding it so tightly her knuckles turned white. 'Then, when that poor young man dropped dead, and— and that girl was taken by the police ... he just ... left.'

Kyra frowned. 'Do you know what he looked like?' she asked, already reaching for her satchel.

The old lady paused. 'It was dark,' she muttered, 'but I do remember catching a small glimpse of his face when the fireworks went off.'

'Can you describe him?' Kyra asked, pulling out a pencil and a small sheet of paper.

The old lady nodded.

After a long while, and a tedious amount of time drawing a portrait, Kyra was headed back to Luca's house, a small sheet of paper held in her hand like a precious jewel. There was a smile on her face, for she felt as if they were finally getting somewhere.

However, as Kyra approached the house, the smile disappeared from her face in a matter of seconds, merging instead into a drawn out gasp.

The door was wide open, and inside, Matteo sat by the

table, his head in his hands.

As Kyra shut the door behind her, Matteo looked up, and the expression he gave her made her heart flip.

'What happened?' she mumbled, although she had already guessed the answer.

'They're gone,' Matteo said, his voice shaking.

'They took Luca and Rosie.'

'The police?' Kyra dreaded the answer. Matteo shook his head. Kyra dropped into a seat beside him, bouncing her knee up and down.

'Did they take Razario?' she asked after a moment's consideration.

Matteo shook his head, gesturing to the stairs.

'I'm not sure what use he'll be in helping us find my son,' he muttered, an edge to his voice. Kyra noticed how quickly his tone had changed.

After hesitating for a moment, she ran upstairs. She found Razario on the windowsill, biting the feathers under his wing.

'Where's Rosie?' she demanded.

'Took your time' he croaked, looking up when she walked in.

'Where is she?' Kyra repeated. She was becoming impatient; she could feel anger rising inside of her, like a cobra, rearing up to its shackles.

'The island,' Razario said, flying onto Kyra's arm.

Kyra frowned, making her way back down the stairs. 'Where?'

Razario was silent for a moment, then he flew over to the window and started tapping his beak persistently against the glass.

'We're late,' he said.

Matteo looked up to the window, then back to Kyra with a hopeful expression.

'Are you sure this is going to work?' he asked.

Kyra shrugged. 'No. but we haven't any other options.'

Matteo nodded, standing up and heading for the door. Razario perched on Kyra's shoulder, pulling at the shoulder of her dress. She frowned at him, brushing his beak away. He responded by digging his claws sharply into her coat. She winced and glared at him, but he wouldn't budge from his position. Sighing, she grabbed her bag and slung it over her other shoulder, following Matteo outside.

'WHO'S LAZARUS?' Rosie demanded. Axle looked startled for the first time.

'Lazarus is an enemy.' he muttered darkly. 'He goes by many names, and many faces, although none change the darkness that plagues his heart.'

Rosie frowned. 'What does that mean?'

Axle drew a long breath. 'Lazarus is a threat to the Lightwings,' he said. 'He wants power, and will stop at nothing to get it.'

Axle looked down at his hands. The pale haze around him vibrated violently, and after a few quiet moments, something appeared in his palms. Rosie expected her hands to pass straight through it as he gave it to her. It was a leather notebook, with a small symbol burned on the front; a crescent moon surrounding a small circle.

'What is this?' Luca gestured to the pattern.

'It's the Lightwing crest.'

Rosie scoffed, but Axle ignored her. 'That coin you have in your hand,' he gestured to her palm. Rosie had forgotten she was still holding it. She glanced down at it and dropped it to the floor. It clattered against the jewels as it fell.

'That belongs to the Lightwings. There are few left, after the incident.'

Rosie frowned. 'What incident?'

Axle did not answer.

'All the answers you need are in here,' he muttered, 'but for now, I must go.'

'Wait!' Rosie tried, reaching her hand out. She gasped when her fingers passed through him. He offered her a small smile, before he disappeared completely, leaving the two of them alone, the purple mist swirling inside the crystal like an angry storm.

'We need to go.' Rosie dashed back out of the chamber and up the stairs, her feet stumbling on the uneven steps, her breath catching in her throat, like a loose piece of string snagging on a bramble.

Luca was by her side in seconds, his fingers enclosed around a small emerald.

Rosie looked at it with raised eyebrows and he shrugged, dropping it into his pocket.

'You have a way out?' he muttered.

Rosie shook her head. Light flooded in through the hole in the top of the cave, which was too high up for them to try and climb out of. In desperation, she grabbed onto the rock and began to lift herself up. It seemed to be working, but when a large chunk of stone crumbled at her touch, she fell back to the ground with an annoyed sigh. She looked over at Luca, who was sitting on the ground, looking up at the hole in the cave.

Rosie glowered at him. 'Are you paying attention?' She demanded. 'Because in case you haven't noticed, we're stuck in a *glowing tunnel* with no way out, while a murderer walks free.'

Luca shrugged. 'We're going to get out.' He pointed his finger upwards. 'See?'

Rosie followed his gaze above, her eyes widening when she saw what he was gesturing to.

'Kyra?!'

'Oh, thank the Heavens!' came Kyra's relieved yell.

'You were starting to get us worried.'

Kyra was soon accompanied by a man, who peered down the edge, his hair falling in front of his eyes.

'Luca?' Matteo called, his voice thick with concern, 'are you alright?'

Luca smiled and waved to his father. 'Perfectly fine,' he said.

Matteo threw down a rope and ran to tie it to the nearest tree.

'Can you pull yourselves up?' Kyra called down, grabbing the rope in her gloved hands. Rosie's eyes widened slightly, and she gestured over to Luca.

'You go first,' she said. Her voice was confident, but her heart hammered against her chest. Luca nodded and gripped the rope with two hands, moving to the edge of the cave, which he used as a wall of the cave as a brace as he pulled himself upwards.

When he reached the top, he swung one leg over the edge and pulled himself up, he nodded down to her and she gripped the rope tight.

By the time Rosie reached the top of the pit, her hands were red from how tightly she had gripped the rope, and the hem of her dress was scuffed, after being scraped repeatedly against the stones.

She lay against the mud, panting.

'How did you find us?' she asked Kyra, once she had caught her breath. Kyra gestured over shoulder at Razario, who was perched on a low hanging branch of a nearby tree

'He must have seen where they took you,' she said, passing the rope to Matteo, who began rolling it up. Rosie nodded, extending her arm for him to perch on. He landed neatly on her shoulder, and she stroked the feathers on his back with her fingertips.

'We'd better get going,' said Matteo, gesturing to a boat that was moored by a bank of grass. It was a little larger than a gondola, but not by much, and it bobbed gently on the surface of the rippling water. Rosie nodded and headed towards it, the notebook Axle had given her lodged deeply in the pocket of her dress.

'We've got a lot to tell you,' she muttered as she clambered into the boat, scrunching up her legs so Luca could fit in front of her. They sat, shoulder to shoulder, as Matteo and Luca began to row. The boat slid forward with a slow, nauseating rhythm. The harsh wind whipped Rosie's hair onto her face, and she blinked it away. Venice was merely a hued silhouette against the heavy rain, large buildings and hazy church spires looming through the mist.

Nobody spoke on the ride back; they wouldn't have been heard over the pelting rain and angry gusts of wind. When they reached the city, Matteo slid his boat into a thin canal and then headed in the direction of his house. Rosie exited the boat cautiously, keeping an eye out for anybody who could be watching her.

Matteo opened the door to his house and they all piled in, dripping water on his carpet. Luca dumped heavy logs on the remains of a fire.

Rosie took a seat by the blaze, warming her hands in front of the flames, which danced in the grate, crackling quietly, sending sparks flying in all directions.

She closed her eyes, piecing together what she and Luca had learned in the cave. She still found Axle and his words hard to believe; they were not in a time of magic and pirates, surely there was a logical explanation for what they had seen.

Bringing the notebook out of her pocket, she studied it in the light of the leaping flames. It was mostly similar to Nico's; the strange, jumbled sentences, the numbers placed in random orders. But as Rosie turned the page, a drawing stuck out. It was faint, the pencil fading from age, but in the dim light of the fire, Rosie smiled.

XIV

QUIET UNCERTAINTIES

ONCE EVERYONE had settled around the fire, warming their hands by the flames, Rosie spoke up.

'Did Gwydion give you any information?' she directed her question at Kyra, who shook her head, her expression bitter. Rosie had already anticipated the outcome; from the few moments she had shared with Kyra's brother, she had gathered that he wasn't the type of person who would pay close attention to details, or get involved in affairs that were none of his own.

'But then I went to see Sofia,' Kyra spoke up, clearing her throat. 'And, reluctant as she was, she told me she'd seen Roberto and Nico speaking the night he died.'

Rosie leaned closer in her chair, intertwining her fingers.

'Sofia said they were talking about someone called Edward ...' Kyra trailed off, looking over at Rosie expectantly.

'Didn't Alvar mention Edward?'

Rosie nodded. 'But as far as we're concerned, he's just a name that keeps reappearing. We have nothing against him ...'

'Maybe not anymore,' Kyra muttered, pulling a sheet of crumpled paper from her bag.

'After a long time thinking, I went to see if anyone had witnessed Roberto's death. I talked to a woman who claimed she saw someone watch you from the shadows.'

Rosie furrowed her brows. Roberto's death was certainly memorable; surely she would have noticed if someone had been watching her. She had been especially alert, watching every building with care.

That was until Enzo appeared.

Rosie's eyes widened.

The coat tails. Of course! She thought she had been imagining things, that it was a simple trick of the light, a shadow moving at an odd angle.

'There *was* someone watching me!' she exclaimed.

Kyra nodded. 'I have a description of him here,' she said triumphantly, as she handed over the paper.

Rosie scanned the image; a long, thin face, mouth twisted into a smirk, and a paper-thin scar that trailed across his left eye.

'I've seen this face before. I think he was the man who attacked me,' she murmured, her voice quiet. She shared a concerned look with Luca, who twisted the ring on his finger nervously.

'Do you suppose he poisoned Roberto?' he asked.

After a moment's hesitation, Rosie nodded.

'I know he did.' She looked up, but was met with confused gazes. Rosie drew a breath to explain.

'Alvar said Nico had worked for Edward, and Roberto must have too, considering they were both talking about him at the party. I think Roberto was murdered when Edward thought he would give away important information.'

'About what?' Kyra asked. Rosie smiled, opening the notebook Axle had given her.

It wasn't anything interesting, weathered and worn-down, pages dry and spotted with age. Most of it was empty, only faint paragraphs of half-written sentences, and sketches that were so pale, they looked as if they had been drawn hundreds of years ago.

Some pages were missing, others ripped and frayed. At the very back of the book, one page had been torn in half, though there was nothing on it to indicate something important had been taken.

The paper crackled dryly as she flicked through to the page she wanted, and placed it on the floor for all to see.

There was a collective gasp as everyone caught on to what she was saying. There was a drawing of a man in the notebook, almost exactly the same as the one Kyra had made of Edward.

Only Edward wasn't the name that was written underneath his face.

It was Lazarus.

XXV

LAZARUS

'THEY'RE THE SAME PERSON!' Luca breathed, picking up the book to examine it further.

Rosie nodded. 'Edward must be one of his aliases.' Everything was beginning to come together in her mind, like a missing puzzle piece, finally fitting into place.

'But why Nico?' Kyra's voice was tentative, as if she feared asking the question.

Rosie looked up again. 'We know he was on the island, from the algae on his key. And we know Lazarus wanted to get there, but couldn't. I think he used Nico to reach the island.'

Luca frowned. 'But even if he did use Nico, why would he then kill him? Surely he needed him instead.'

Rosie nodded. 'Maybe Nico learned something. Something he decided not to share. Maybe Lazarus had him killed because he discovered what he shouldn't have.'

'But this is all going off a hunch,' Matteo said, resting his chin on his palm. 'You don't really have much proof.'

Rosie sighed. Although she hated to admit it, Matteo was right. Throwing accusations would do nothing to convince the police if there was no proof to back it up, and at the moment,

they only had the word of three teenagers and an ancient –
not to mention semi-transparent – priest.

Rosie huffed in annoyance. She stayed silent for a moment,
until she felt Razario tugging on her hair.

She glared at him but he continued to pull at her, then
thrust his wing towards the stairs.

Rosie gave him a confused look, before grinning and
dashing to where he had pointed. As she grabbed Nico's
notebook from her room, Rosie found it hard to understand
why Lazarus hadn't taken it with him.

'Look at this,' she muttered, once she was back downstairs.
She flicked through the pages quickly, her fingers catching the
rough edge of the paper as she skimmed through the book.
On the last page, there was a map, scrawled messily in dark red
ink; something Rosie had somehow missed until now.

'This leads to the island,' she said, running her finger over
the blotches of stained ink, to a small dot marked with a
black cross.

'But we already know he was at the island, Rosie,' Luca
mumbled, his voice low. She fell silent as Luca took the book
from her hands and flicked through, his brow furrowing as his
eyes scanned the pages.

He was about to close the book when something fell out of
it, dropping soundlessly to the floor.

He frowned and picked it up. 'What's this?' He handed it
to Rosie, who unfolded it slowly.

'I'm not sure,' she said in a quiet voice, reading the flowing
letters:

"I have stumbled into something far out of my control.
He wants more than he should have. He is too hungry for it.
He will do more than what is necessary. But he knows that
I'm hiding something from him. I likely don't have long left.

Lazarus knows where I am. When he finds me, he will kill me. I only hope he doesn't uncover what he is searching for. God help us all if he does.

It was signed with Nico's name, and the words seemed to echo around Rosie's thoughts. How had she not found this before? Surely it hadn't slipped past her. Had she really just not noticed it?

She dropped the paper on the floor as realisation formed in her mind.

'We have to tell the police!' she demanded, standing up and heading to the door. Before she could leave, however, Luca pushed her back into her chair.

'You can't go,' he reminded her. 'The police are still looking for you, and if they catch you this time, you won't get out as easily as before.'

Rosie sighed heavily and crossed her arms. 'Then you can go,' she suggested, glaring at him. 'They've already met Kyra, so you're our only option.'

He sighed and looked at his father, who hesitated for a moment, before giving a defeated shrug.

'Alright,' he said, leaning forward in his chair. 'But we must think of a better way to approach this. You can't simply flounce into the place and demand that the police catch a suspect they don't even know exists.'

Rosie nodded and looked down, twisting the ring on her finger as she thought. She wondered if there was a way of finding and confronting Lazarus, without anyone discovering her.

Opening the notebook Axle had given her, she trailed her fingertips down the edges of the crackling pages.. She opened it to the page with Lazarus's picture, her eyes scanning the words that were written underneath:

Lazarus Sicklebeak followed in the footsteps of his family, seeking power and wealth. Nobody is sure what he wants, only that he has been searching for the Lightwings' treasure for years. Alfred Lightwing discovered that he was leading a group of people to hunt for the treasure. Fortunately, Lazarus has been unsuccessful so far in his pursuit, but with his family history, it is safe to assume that he will stop at nothing to get what he wants.

Alfred has tracked Lazarus and his team to the Ponte delle Guglie, in Venice. Sources say they meet at this point regularly.

Rosie stayed silent for a moment, as the smoky uncertainties in her mind solidified into a conclusion.

She grinned.

'I have a plan,' she said.

TWO HOURS LATER, Luca knocked on the heavy wooden door of detective Enzo's office, gripping the note Nico had written between his fingers. As he waited for someone to open the door, everything he and Rosie had gone over spun around in his mind, like a dog chasing its tail. He knew what he had to do, but he still wasn't convinced it would work. No matter how many times he had gone over the plan, he was sure something was bound to go wrong. Although he trusted Rosie, he believed she was rushing into it too quickly, forgetting what they were up against. She seemed to be enjoying it too much, almost as if it were a game.

Luca was drawn out of his thoughts as the office door opened. A policeman stood behind it, glancing down at him under the wide brim of his hat.

'May I help you?' he asked, his voice in a tone that made Luca feel as if he didn't fancy helping anybody.

'Actually, you may.' Luca walked into Enzo's office and sat

down, crossing his legs.

'I'm here to tell you who *really* murdered Nico Lombardi.' He kept his voice calm and his gaze fixed as he spoke.

Enzo raised his eyebrows, but did not sit down. 'I already know,' he said. 'It was Rosie Lightwing.'

Luca shook his head. 'I'm afraid not,' he said, 'Rosie didn't commit either of the crimes.'

Enzo frowned. 'And how would you know that?' he demanded sceptically, finally taking a seat.

'That's not important. What you need to know is this.'

He handed Enzo the piece of paper with Nico's confession on it. Enzo read it slowly, his eyes trailing from side to side as he studied the words.

'This ... this is fake,' he muttered after a long pause.

Luca shook his head. 'No it's not; you've simply been chasing the wrong person.

He leaned over and passed Enzo the drawing of Lazarus.

'This is the man you're looking for. He'll be on the Ponte delle Guglie tonight. I suggest you bring a couple of officers with you when you go. He's dangerous.'

Enzo frowned angrily and grabbed his wrist. 'Have you been in contact with Miss Lightwing?' he demanded.

Luca hesitated.

Enzo huffed. 'Withholding information from us could end in dire consequences. I ought to arrest you where you stand.'

Luca pulled his wrist from Enzo's grip. 'I'm not who you should be worrying about,' he said, his voice calm despite the thrashing of his heart against his chest.

'Just be on that bridge tonight.'

Luca didn't wait for an answer, he ran from Enzo's office with his hand buried deep in his coat pocket.

XXVI

HUNTER

'ARE YOU SURE this is going to work?' asked Kyra, tightening the laces of Rosie's corset.

'No,' Rosie sucked in a sharp breath as the corset tightened around her ribcage.

'But it's the best plan we've got.'

Kyra nodded and tied the laces into a neat bow, pulling the back of Rosie's dress up further and connecting it together with buttons.

Rosie smiled at her, pulling her mask over her eyes.

It was dark red, to match her floor-length dress, which had long sleeves and lace edges; and small, amber buttons running down to the bottom of her waist. Kyra had given it to her, and though Rosie agreed it was beautiful, she had never felt more constricted in her life. She wasn't one to wear fancy dresses, or high heels, and now, possibly at the most inconvenient time, she was forced to dress up for the Carnival, in tight, restricting clothes. Looking beside her, she noticed that Kyra didn't seem at all fazed by her costume.

'Doesn't wearing this bother you?' she asked, trying to pull the tight sleeves of her dress away from her skin.

Kyra shook her head. 'Not really. Father always has important people around, so I'm forced to dress up as elegantly as possible.'

Taking a better look at her, Rosie decided that *elegant* was the perfect word to describe Kyra's looks.

Her long, light teal dress reached the ground, covering the black heels she moved so effortlessly in. Her sleeves were shorter than Rosie's, with a slight puff in them, and she wore ivory gloves that reached just below her elbow. Her long blonde hair was pulled back in a bun, and the few strands that fell out were curled, framing her face, which was covered in a thin layer of makeup.

Kyra caught Rosie staring at her and blushed, hiding her face behind a lace fan.

'Are you ready?' Rosie asked, Kyra nodded, putting on a mask of her own, a blue eye-covering with a large white feather erupting from the top.

'I really hope you know what you're doing ...' she muttered nervously, heading for the door.

'Don't worry,' Rosie replied cheerfully. 'What's the worst that could happen?'

She looked up at Kyra, who must have started to say something, for she looked down quickly, twiddling her fingers with anxious movements.

Rosie laughed and patted her on the back. She opened the door and stepped outside.

The cold wind was like a knife in her throat, and she sucked in a sharp breath of air, wrapping her arms around herself as she walked down the cobbled road, Kyra following close behind her, a gloved hand wrapped around the beaded strap of her purse.

Silhouettes of looming buildings peeked through a thick

blanket of mist, hazy shapes against the darkening sky. Street lamps casted blurred reflections on the slick roads, and in the distance, fireworks sent bursts of colours scattering against the sky.

The bridge was small, despite its width, and the two halves of it created a point as they met in the middle. Its stone ledge was held together by short, pointed pillars, and at the edges, two large white posts towered above them.

Rosie kept her eyes peeled as she walked to the edge of the bridge. Although there wasn't much point; she could barely see through the crowds of people. Standing next to Kyra, she leant against the railing, her eyes fixed on the canal in front of her.

The stone pressed bitterly against her palm. A barely healed cut lay there, from when she had fallen into the cave. She winced, and pulled back to examine it.

It wasn't as bad as she had initially thought, though it still stung against the icy breeze

She closed her hands into loose fists and turned her attention back to the canal.

In the night, the water held more mystery and surprise, like a cloth hiding an unknown object. It was just a rippling surface of darkness, lit only by the street lamps and the glow of the rising moon. Hazy reflections of boats, and people walking on the cobbles drifted across its surface like ghosts, and though it was barely noticeable, dark algae swirled at the bottom of the water.

On other occasions, Rosie could have stood there for hours, watching the water ripple from her spot on the bridge. But not tonight. Tonight, she had to be watchful, to keep her gaze fixed around her instead of in front. She had to pay attention to each person on the bridge, to every costume and every mask, every face, and every huddle of people.

After what felt like hours, they were joined by a boy with long hair and a dashing smile.

'Hello,' Luca muttered, leaning his arms against the stone, shuffling closer to Rosie and giving her a small grin.

She smiled back, keeping her eyes level with his. From behind her, Kyra chuckled quietly.

'Did it work?' she asked Luca.

He gave a hesitant nod. 'I think so.'

Rosie's heart pounded in her chest, and she took a deep breath to steady herself, closing her eyes.

After a while, the bridge had emptied of people and they were left alone, the three of them gazing out at the water. 'Rosie,' Kyra whispered, pointing her finger to the end of the bridge. 'Look.'

Rosie's gaze followed Kyra's fingers, her eyes narrowing. There were three men huddling close to each other, their heads bent low as they talked.

'Do you suppose that's them?' Luca asked. Rosie leaned closer. It was difficult to make out their faces in the darkness, but from the pale glow of the moon, something stood out; a thin sliver of a scar, half-hidden by a hooked mask, that made his shadow look as if he really did have a beak.

'That's them.' Rosie took a small step forward, her eyes fixed.

'What do we do now?' Kyra whispered.

'Just listen,' she breathed.

They fell silent, leaning forward to listen to the conversation that played between the three men.

'And you're certain she won't be a bother to us any longer?' Lazarus was asking. His voice was rough, like gravel, his tone unforgiving.

'We dumped them both on the island,' another man spoke. Rosie recognised his voice as the tattooed man from the ship.

'They're likely to starve,' he continued.

Lazarus nodded his head approvingly.

A long pause followed, filled only with the loud chatter of tourists, and the soft lapping of water against the stone ledges.

'Yet we're no closer to finding a way into that blasted cave.' Lazarus' voice was gritty, as if he was only daring them to contradict him.

The two men shook their heads.

Rosie grinned to herself in the dark, and continued listening.

Lazarus sighed. Beside him, the tattooed man spoke up. His voice was desperate as he scrambled for an excuse.

'We can keep looking. We won't stop until—' his words were cut short when Lazarus held up a hand.

He moved his finger to where Rosie was standing, and for a moment, he seemed to freeze. He lowered his hand and stepped closer.

'What would three children like yourselves be doing here on such a fine night, so far away from the festivities?' he asked, his voice steely.

Rosie stepped closer. He was almost daring her to do so.

'Just enjoying the view,' she replied. Lazarus chuckled.

'You ... are a *terrible* liar, Miss Lightwing,' he said, and although she could only see his eyes, Rosie knew he was smiling.

She opened her mouth to speak, but Lazarus had already turned on his heels, and walked briskly down the bridge, the two men following close behind him. There was something in the way Lazarus walked – not a single note of hesitation or nervousness.

He knew Rosie would follow him.

Lazarus paused for a moment, but only to gesture to the men by his side. They shared a glance, before trudging away, lurking in the shadows of a cramped alleyway.

Rosie stepped forward, but Luca grabbed her arm.

'What are you doing?' he hissed, 'you know it's a trap!'

'I don't care!' Rosie spat back, pulling free of his grip. 'He;s a murderer!'

Luca sighed, and beside him, Kyra shook her head.

'You're going to get yourself killed,' she muttered, as Lazarus strode closer to the edge of the bridge.

'I'm well aware of the risks, just ... stick to what we agreed on.'

Rosie didn't allow the conversation to continue further, turning on her heel and chasing after Lazarus at full pelt.

He wasn't too far ahead, and it didn't take long for Rosie to reach him. He turned his head, and Rosie's eyes met with his cold stare, gazing at her from behind his slick hooked mask.

'You're far too predictable, Miss Lightwing.' His voice was icy, and a shiver ran down Rosie's spine.

Before she could reply, however, he had sped up, dashing through crowds of gathering people and into bustling courtyards. It didn't take a second thought for Rosie to chase after him, skidding and stumbling against uneven stones that jutted out of the path. Lazarus sped past a chattering group of people and into a large stone building, slamming the door behind him so hard that the glass rattled in its frame.

Rosie tore through the entrance after him, her hair falling in front of her face, panting heavily. Ahead of her, the tail of Lazarus' black coat disappeared behind a door. The moment Rosie entered the room, bright lights hit her face, like a harsh gust of wind. The room was large, occupied with people in sparkling dresses and tailored suits, jewellery and cufflinks, that glittered off the chandelier hanging from the tiled ceiling. The slow tinkling of a piano came from somewhere in the back of the room, echoing into the space. In the middle of the room, couples twirled and swayed in time to the music, while others lingered by the edges, looking almost longingly at the effortless dancing.

Rosie's eyes searched frantically, but Lazarus' leather coat had disappeared, drowning in a sea of black suits and shining masks. Rosie grabbed the shoulder of a man in a dark suit, but when he spun round, he gave her a confused look and frowned at her behind his dark red mask.

'Can I help you with something, Miss?' he asked.

Rosie shook her head and turned away from him, glimpsing another leather coat vanishing behind a woman in a wide ball gown. Rosie raced forward, but before she reached the man, someone grabbed her arm in a tight grip. She let out a quiet yelp as she was dragged to the middle of the room. Rosie looked up, and her gaze met with Lazarus' icy stare.

His eyes grinned at her.

'You were beginning to panic, Miss Lightwing,' he muttered, as he clutched her waist. Rosie stiffened, flinching away, but he grabbed her hand and moved it to rest on his shoulder.

She was vaguely aware of a slow waltz playing in the background, though she could barely hear it over the pounding of her frantic heart against her ribcage.

Lazarus began to move to the music, pulling Rosie's unresponsive body with him.

'What are you doing?' she hissed, though her voice sounded a lot quieter than she had intended it to be.

Lazarus shrugged. 'Dancing, of course.'

Rosie rolled her eyes at his nonchalance.

'I must admit, Miss Lightwing, I wasn't expecting to hear from you again.'

Rosie swallowed. 'You underestimated me.'

Lazarus chuckled, a deep, gravelly chuckle. 'I suppose I did. I should have known better. You are a Lightwing, after all.'

She winced when his grip tightened around her palm, pressing against her barely healed cut.

He looked down to her hand, eyes narrowed.

'That looks painful,' he said, almost to himself.

Rosie didn't reply. She felt frozen in place, unable to move from his effortlessly strong hold.

'I'm prepared to answer your questions,' he said.

Rosie hated how level his tone was, as if he was completely unfazed by the entire event.

'You're acting like this is just a game!' Rosie exclaimed, anger laced through her voice.

'Everything is a game, Miss Lightwing. It just depends on who's willing to play.'

She stiffened. 'And I suppose Nico wasn't,' she muttered.

Lazarus laughed. It was a short laugh, almost as if he couldn't force it to last any longer. He let go of her waist and lifted his arm, as she twirled underneath it, returning to rest in his vice-tight grip with a grimace.

'You are terribly mistaken, my dear,' Lazarus said, 'Nico was as willing as they got. He was, unfortunately, playing the wrong game.'

'So you had him killed.' Rosie's voice was bitter. Lazarus shrugged. 'I did what had to be done.'

As Rosie opened her mouth to speak, the music in the background faded to a close. Lazarus stepped back, letting go of her waist and giving her a short bow. Rosie offered him a halfhearted curtsey, refusing to take her eyes off him.

'It's a shame to cut our conversation short, Miss Lightwing, but I must be on my way.'

Lazarus didn't wait another moment, before turning on his heels and dashing through the room, pushing past a crowd of people. A collective group of annoyed exclamations and loud gasps erupted from the room, as Rosie chased after Lazarus at full pelt, past the open door and back onto the street.

A gust of cold wind hit her face and she blinked into the rain, as, ahead of her, Lazarus sprinted past watching tourists, pushing them out of his way.

Angry shouts followed him almost as quickly as Rosie did, chasing him through cramped alleyways and across crumbling stone bridges.

XXVII

HUNTED

KYRA CHEWED ON HER NAILS restlessly, her eyes set on the building Rosie had just ran into. She could feel her stomach twisting with anxiousness, and her heart thrashing against her chest.

'I hate this,' she muttered, almost too quiet for Luca to hear. He nodded, leaning against the railing of the bridge. He dropped his gaze to the canal, watching the water absentmindedly.

'She's thought about this,' he said, though his voice didn't sound very confident.

'She'll be okay.'

Kyra wasn't so sure. She had not spent much time with Rosie, but she knew her to be the type who rushed into things without entirely thinking them through. Though Kyra admired Rosie's bravery, she was concerned that her rash decisions would get her into serious trouble.

After all, her actions *had* caused her to be wrongly accused of murder, and taken to a faraway island by a man she was now chasing into a building, alone.

Kyra had a dreaded feeling that Rosie may not escape so easily this time.

She sighed and rocked back on her heels. If she weren't so nervous about the events of the evening, she would have taken the chance to reflect on the fact that, for once, her father wasn't beside her, watching and commenting on her every move. She had caught herself looking over her shoulder multiple times that evening, just to make sure he wasn't following her. She wasn't used to being outside her house; her entire childhood consisted of scheduled lessons with a tutor she deeply disliked, and hours of reading complicated books with overly descriptive explanations. She never had the chance to explore the city, despite having lived in it for over three years.

She looked to her side, where Luca's father was approaching them, eyebrows furrowed.

He stood next to Luca and followed his unmoving gaze.

'Any reason why that particular building is so interesting?' he asked.

Luca nodded, though he didn't avert his eyes.

'She's in there with Lazarus,' he said.

Matteo nodded. 'Seems like a good idea. He's only a murderer, of course she should be in there alone.'

Kyra swallowed. 'She has a plan. And the police should be here soon.'

Matteo frowned, but nodded after a moment's pause.

They stood in silence, focused intently on what was happening around them; the chattering crowds, filing in and out of bustling houses, the canal, rippling against the gentle wind, the voices drifting past them, as they waited by the edge of the bridge.

For a long time, nothing happened. And then everything happened.

Kyra heard loud voices and angry exclamations, and turned her head to the noise. On the far side of the building they had just been watching, the door had burst open, and two people had run out.

Kyra's eyes widened. Although it was dark, and the figures were far away, she knew instantly who they were.

'There!' she pointed to the figures, who were now hidden behind a group of old houses.

She and Luca shared a worried look, but before either of them could follow, Matteo stopped them.

'You can't go,' he said, though he didn't sound too sure about his own statement.

Luca shook his head. 'He's a murderer, you said it yourself!'

He grabbed Kyra's wrist and pulled her along beside him, as they chased after Rosie, who had disappeared into the shadows.

ROSIE FOLLOWED LAZARUS, slipping and stumbling, her dress catching against the floor. Lazarus reached the edge of a building, where he gripped the rungs of a rusty ladder and began to pull himself up, Rosie close at his heels.

His pace slowed, and soon she was only metres behind him. Lazarus turned to her. In the dark, his silhouette seemed to melt into the gloom, lit up only by the occasional firework or lazy sliver of moonlight that peeked through passing clouds.

Lazarus paused, then pulled something out of his coat. It was a knife, long and thin, with a bone handle and a sharp point that seemed to taunt Rosie, daring her to make a move. Lazarus lunged forward.

Without thinking, she dodged sideways and stuck out her foot. Lazarus stepped over her neatly and stood up straight.

'You're quick on your feet ... Unlike your *poor* grandfather.'

Rosie's stomach dropped, and she froze in her spot.

'What?' she whispered, in a voice that sounded a thousand miles away.

'I suppose you were still hoping he would be around. Alas, his old age failed him when we fought. A shame, really, I was hoping for more of a competition.'

Rosie clenched her eyes shut, refusing to let the desperate tears spill. She lunged forward, grabbing Lazarus's arm and pulling him onto the stone. He laughed as he hit the ground, shoving Rosie off him and pushing her down, bringing the knife closer to her chest. Lazarus's face was so close to hers, she could smell the smoke on his breath. Rosie groaned and pushed him off her, standing up and moving her feet into a stronger position.

Lazarus ran, dashing over the stone roof, pausing slightly at the edge, then jumping onto the next building. Rosie chased after him, but came to an abrupt halt when her dress caught underneath her. She sighed angrily and ripped the side of the fabric, causing a long slit to appear in the skirt. Then, she jumped, her feet leaving the ground and landing softly on the other side.

When she looked up, however, Lazarus was nowhere in sight. Rosie frowned and inched closer. In the dark, she could barely see her own hand in front of her face.

Then, a firework went off. Blue and crimson splattered across the sky, like paint on a dark canvass, and a loud bang echoed into the night.

The flash lit up the sky, and a sudden figure loomed in front of her, a soft outline of a hooked beak mere inches away from her face.

Rosie let out a loud gasp and jolted backwards, but Lazarus was already advancing.

Under the moon, the tip of his blade shimmered.

Then, and much to her surprise, Lazarus stumbled. He threw his hands in the air and gave a grunt of displeasure, and from his cloak, a small chain flew out. It had a disc on the end of it, though in the dark, Rosie couldn't make out what was engraved on its front.

From above, Razario lurched forwards. Rosie grinned.

Taking her chance, she hopped down onto the roof of a lower building and scrambled to find cover behind a chimney.

It had only occurred to her what was happening, as she leaned against the stone, trying to regulate her breathing; she was no longer following Lazarus; he was *hunting* her.

She heard the crack of tiles breaking, and she knew he was near. She held her breath, pressing herself as close to the stone as possible. She could hear footsteps, and heavy breathing. Rosie inched forward, inclining her head round the end of the chimney. Even in the dark, she knew there was nobody there.

She breathed out a quiet sigh of relief, hoping he had moved to search for her somewhere else.

She turned back, and screamed.

He was inches away from her, waiting, like a cat watching its prey. His hooked mask was almost pressing against her skin.

She scrambled back, her hand slipping off the edge of the building. She let out a short yell as she dropped down, landing harshly on an inclining roof. She winced, and struggled for balance, as Lazarus hopped neatly down in front of her. She backed away.

'You really don't give up,' he said as he corrected himself, tucking his loose chain back under his clothes. 'Just like dear old Alfred.'

'Stop talking,' Rosie spat, throwing a punch at his head, which he ducked neatly, chuckling.

She moved to the side as he extended his knife once more,

but just a second too late, for the blade caught on the sleeve of her dress, ripping it in two, grazing her arm. She cried out when her skin tore, jolting backwards.

Something in Lazarus' eyes changed when he saw her blood on the blade of his knife. He paused for a moment.

Razario flew down to flap and scratch at him, but his attacks were unsuccessful. Lazarus waved him away with angry hands, swinging his knife in the air, so that Razario was forced to shrink back.

Lazarus bent down beside Rosie and leaned closer. She hit him hard on the face, but he didn't stumble. Instead, he grabbed her jaw and forced her to look at him.

'You are a fool, Rosie,' he stated. Her blood ran cold at how easily he spoke her name.

'And you have stumbled into my trap.'

Rosie scoffed, pulling her face away from him, though he inched closer with every breath he took.

'We both knew I'd follow you,' Rosie panted, 'not much of a trap, really.'

Lazarus shook his head. 'You are as naive as your grandfather.'

Rosie clenched her jaw and inched backwards. Behind the beak of his mask, Lazarus was grinning. He leaned forward and grabbed her arm. She winced.

'Do you think you simply *stumbled* upon Nico's body? You still believe that you just ... *missed* the note explaining who had him killed? You expect me to be foolish enough to leave you on the island with your ancestor's findings?'

His voice rose in pitch with each statement.

Rosie froze. She tried to speak, but her words only came out as a whisper. She swallowed and shook her head.

'You—'

She could only manage a single word, before her voice was drowned out by the sound of rapidly approaching footsteps. She looked up, her vision blurry.

Behind Lazarus, Luca and Matteo were advancing towards her, closely followed by Kyra, who's hair was in disarray.

A faint grin tugged at her lips when she heard Luca call her name.

She wrenched her arm from Lazarus' tight grip and stumbled to her feet. She was lightheaded and shaking.

Lazarus looked back, and for a single fleeting second, he didn't move. He stood still, watching. He glanced at Rosie with narrowed eyes. She stepped backwards, her shoe hanging off the rooftop edge.

Then, Lazarus moved. In one swift moment, he hit her hard on the temple. She staggered backwards, vision blurry. She heard voices, though they were muffled and heavy, as if she were underwater. She felt someone grab at her arms, as her knees buckled. She was faintly aware of more footsteps, though she couldn't tell if they were leaving or accroaching. She tried to will herself to move, but her limbs felt like lead, and her head ached terribly.

She knew someone was calling her name, but her blurred vision made it almost impossible to see what was happening; she could only piece together vague silhouettes and shadowy figures.

From somewhere high above, the moon's brightness was faltering, shivering and fading into nothing more than shadow, that shrouded her in darkness.

XXVIII

THE FINAL PIECE

THE SOUND OF SEAGULLS woke Rosie from a troubled sleep. Her head ached, and she sat up groggily, rubbing a hand over her eyes. She could still feel the cold stone against her cheek, and the steel grip of Lazarus' hand on her face. She shivered. From the windowsill, Razario gave her a loud croak. She smiled and walked over to stroke the feathers under his beak.

'Back from the dead?' he teased. She frowned.

She couldn't have been asleep for more than a few hours ... could she?

She sighed and got dressed, noting that her arm was wrapped tightly in a bandage, and a cloth covered her left hand. She headed downstairs, the floorboards creaking under her careful footsteps. As she approached the bottom of the stairs, the sound of voices became clear. She swung the door open and they all abruptly stopped speaking, heads turning to look at her. Luca and his father were sitting opposite Agatha, who was in an armchair by the fire. On the floor, Kyra sat, cross-legged, a pencil behind her ear.

'Morning,' Rosie muttered in a quiet voice.

Luca grinned and stood up from his seat, walking over to her and throwing his arm around her shoulder.

'How are you feeling?' Kyra questioned, looking up from a drawing she had been working on.

Rosie wasn't sure how she felt, after finding out that the whole investigation had been a trap she had waltzed carelessly into. She offered a small shrug and a half-hearted smile. She walked to the kitchen and poured herself a glass of water, which did little to soothe her paper-dry throat.

'Rosie, sit.' Matteo stood up and offered her his chair.

'I see that you've managed to put your self defence to good use.' He chuckled, and Rosie wasn't sure if he was joking or not.

'I have a good teacher,' she said, sitting down and glancing at Agatha, who smiled at her.

'Hello Rosie,' she said drily. 'Glad to see you're not dead.'

Rosie nodded, unable to think of something to say back.

'Me too,' she said at last, looking down.

'Want to know what happened with Lazarus?' Luca asked. Rosie nodded eagerly, only to be met with shaking heads.

Luca hesitated. 'It's bad news ... he escaped from the police.'

'What?!' Rosie snapped her head round to look at him.

'He escaped from the police station the night they caught him,' Kyra continued, bending her head back down to continue sketching. 'They searched everywhere, but couldn't find him. They think he left Venice.'

Rosie sighed and looked down. There was a long silence, in which the last thing Lazarus had said echoed in her mind. She hesitated, before explaining what he had told her, keeping her gaze stuck on the floor until she'd finished. When she looked up again, she couldn't meet anyone's eyes, somehow ashamed that she let herself be fooled so easily.

'But if he wanted the island, why go through all the

trouble?' Luca asked once she'd finished talking.

For the first time, Rosie couldn't think of anything to say. The room filled with a heavy silence.

'At least you're not a criminal anymore,' Kyra tried. 'They linked Nico's handwriting on the note to something he'd written previously. Decided that was enough evidence to place Lazarus under suspicion of both murders.'

Rosie frowned. She didn't believe the police were short-sighted enough to use a piece of evidence that could have been forged, and arrest someone they had never even heard of. But Rosie wasn't a suspect in a murder case anymore, so she let it go.

'... what now?' Kyra asked in a whisper, looking over at Rosie expectantly.

'I just have one more question.' Rosie turned to face Agatha.

'Who are you expecting to show up?' Agatha didn't answer; instead she looked down at her wrinkled hands and fell silent.

'What *are* you talking about?' Luca asked, running a hand through his hair.

'On the first day I started investigating, I noticed how Agatha jumped every time I entered the room, and how she stayed up late, always looking out the window. And I have to ask, who are you waiting for?'

Agatha looked up and smiled. 'Your grandmother, actually.'

Rosie flinched back in surprise, her eyes widening. 'What?' Her voice was barely above a whisper.

'You heard me. I saw the coin in your bag, and I knew this was something to do with your grandparents.'

Rosie had almost forgotten about the coin. After everything else that had happened, it didn't seem like an important detail anymore. She walked over to the door and pulled out her bag. As she picked it up, she could feel her heart drop.

The notebook was gone.

She had placed it there the night before, along with the coin, and a jewel she had taken from the island, just to make sure it was real.

Both the coin and the jewel were still there, sitting loosely on the bottom of the bag, along with a small scrap of paper.

Rosie picked it up with care, hands trembling. The writing was so old fashioned, it looked as if it had been written hundreds of years ago. The curling black letters seemed to imprint themselves into Rosie's mind.

Be more careful, Rosie.
Not everything is always as it seems.
L

Rosie took a slow breath and closed her eyes.

'The notebook is gone,' she said. Her voice was quiet, and the silence she was met with made her wonder if she'd even spoken at all.

'Why?'

Kyra's question, although expected, was not one Rosie could answer. She crumpled Lazarus' note in her hand and sat back down. She shrugged wordlessly. She thought about Axle, and his small mention of 'the incident.' He had told her all the answers to it would be in the notebook, and with it gone, she would never understand what they were, or why the coin was so important to the Lightwings' themselves.

'Lazarus has been one step ahead of us the entire time. Last night was a bait, a distraction, just so he could get what he really wanted.'

Luca frowned. 'What *is* that exactly?'

'I'm not sure ...' she trailed off and looked down at her hands.

She was missing something.

Her fingertips traced over the rough fabric that covered her palm. She remembered Lazarus' reaction to her cut; how his eyes had narrowed, and his movements had slowed just for a split second. The way his voice deepened when he had pointed it out. She shivered. She thought back to the rooftop, when his knife had skimmed against her arm. The short bark of a laugh he had let out, upon seeing her blood on his shimmering blade. She thought of the island, the jewels, the priest, the crystal that glowed after she had touched it—

'Lazarus wanted my blood,' she said at last, her voice cold and quiet, as if she were talking to herself.

Nobody answered for a long moment. Rosie didn't want to meet their shocked gazes. She wished she was wrong, that the triumph in his eyes was from the simple fact that he had hurt her, that the cut on her hand had nothing to do with the crystal's strange abilities, or that the notebook had been stolen for a different reason.

She turned to Luca. 'Remember the crystal?'

He nodded. 'It's hard to forget.'

'It started glowing after I'd touched it. At first I thought it was just a coincidence, or even that I had imagined the entire thing, but now Lazarus has the notebook, and he cut my arm last night, and—' the words were spilling out her mouth, faster than she could comprehend. She could feel her heart pounding against her chest.

'Why on earth would he need your blood?' Kyra's voice was incredulous.

'To get to the cave,' Luca said quietly. 'We know Rosie can get in and he can't. Maybe there's something in there that he wants.'

Rosie's thoughts ran wildly inside her mind, like a deer being chased by its prey. She leaned back a little, closing her eyes.

Lazarus was likely long gone by now. There would be no chance of catching him on the island. And he was smarter than she was. He knew she would figure it out eventually; he wouldn't waste time.

She stood up and brushed down her skirt.

'I'm going to the island,' she said, matter-of-factly.

'You won't find him,' Matteo said.

'I know. But I might be able to discover what he wanted.'

Luca nodded and headed for the door, Kyra following closely, tucking a pencil behind her ear. Razario flew over to perch on Rosie's shoulder. She smiled.

The cold wind was an odd comfort against her skin, as she stepped outside. She grinned faintly.

Although Lazarus had gotten the better of her, she knew she would be seeing him again. And next time, she would not be so easily fooled.

EPILOGUE

FOOTPRINTS AND BLOODSTAINS

THE BOAT MOVED *in a slow, sickening rhythm, the water below it rippling and caving under its weight, as the island drew closer. The boat halted and the man stepped off, his shoe sinking into a wet patch of trampled grass.*

He reached for his rope and tied the boat to an upturned tree root, that jutted out of the ground, like a beetle stuck on its back.

The man continued, his shoes now coated in a thin layer of mud. He looked down to see footprints stamped into the ground.

He smirked. He was in the right place.

Ahead of him, the trees were losing their battle against the ever-growing wind, bending and twisting with the harsh breeze. Raindrops coated the rustling leaves, tumbling off them like hot wax down a tablecloth.

He pushed through the thicket determinedly, brushing away the shrubs that ventured too close to his face.

After a few moments of walking, he came to standstill beside the edge of a large pit. Torn grasses and broken pieces of wood lay in splinters around it, littering the mud.

The man's face split into a wide grin. He pulled a coil of rope from his coat pocket and latched it tightly to the nearest tree.

Once satisfied, he used the rope to lower himself into the pit, dropping neatly to the ground and brushing himself off with a small smirk.

The walls around him were grey, and smelt old, like the inside of an unused cupboard, or an old room that had never been lived in. The uneven floor led him into a thinner section of the tunnel, where stalactites loomed threateningly close to his head, and rocks jutted from the irregular ground. He continued with purpose, until the tunnel opened up to a staircase, carved shallowly into the walls.

There was a cave at the bottom of the stairs, and the man's eyes were instantly drawn to the crystal that stood on a large pedestal in its centre. It was dull, but a light purple mist swayed in the middle of it, almost rippling, like the ocean on a windless day.

All was silent as the man descended into the cave, almost as if the world was holding its breath.

A grin split his face the moment he stepped inside, and he instantly moved over to the crystal.

The man glanced around him. The cave was covered in riches, silver beads and trinkets, old carvings or wooden boxes engraved with gold, jewellery and gems spilling out of them. He picked up a coin from the ground. It was small, yet it seemed to weigh down his palm. He dropped it to the floor a moment later. He didn't like the way the metal almost burned his skin, as if it knew he wasn't worthy of holding it.

He shook himself. He had to hurry. She would soon figure out where he was.

She was smart, smarter than any other Lightwing he had come across. Yet she did not understand how far he would go to get what he wanted.

The man dropped to his knees and pulled something out from his coat. It was a notebook, worn down and tattered with overuse. The leather was frayed and torn in places, the pages dry and spotted with age. There was a symbol burned into the dark chestnut cover; a thin crescent moon surrounding a small hole.

The man traced his fingertip over the image, his eyes flashing. He pulled the cord that tied the covers together and flipped through the pages. They crackled and snapped as he flicked to the end.

In the almost-darkness, he could only make out blotchy words and blurry images. He turned to the back of the book, where there lay half a torn page, barely clinging to the binding. It was empty, but the man was not rattled. Instead, he pulled a small bottle from his pocket.

A thin, almost unnoticeable layer of blood shimmered on the bottom of the glass. The man removed the cork and placed a single, insignificant drop onto the crystal.

For a small, rigid moment, nothing happened.

And then, the crystal lit up. It was almost blinding, and the man was forced to drop his head and squeeze his eyes shut.

The light dimmed after a strained minute of waiting, and the man looked up once more. The purple mist in the crystal was moving a little more rapidly, pulsing like an irregular heartbeat.

The man averted his gaze to the torn page, where images had now appeared under the light. Though only half the paper was visible, the man knew what it was. He grinned, holding it further up to the pale glow. Small clusters of wobbly land clumps and dotted lines littered the page, cut off by the frayed edges of the torn parchment.

The man let out a triumphant bark of a laugh.

He was one step closer to getting all that he wanted.

And nothing would stand in his way.

TO BE CONTINUED...

ACKNOWLEDGEMENTS

I OWE MY BIGGEST THANKS to Leon Conrad, who is the reason this novel is complete. Without your wonderful and inspiring tuition over the past few years, I would not have loved writing nearly as much as I do now.

Thank you to John Martineau for publishing this book and helping me make concrete steps towards my dream career.

A huge thanks to my family, especially my dad, who inspired me to start writing in the first place, encouraging me when I was sure it was going to be a dead end, and for designing and creating the wonderful cover, along with my mum.

Thank you to my beta readers Amelie, Jemimah, Jaia, Lila, Carol and Archie. Without you, this book would have only been an idea in a 14-year-old's mind.

Thank you to everyone who has supported me on social media, your encouraging comments and enthusiasm is the reason why I continue writing.

And thank you to anyone who picked up this book and decided to read it. I am forever grateful.

There's more to come.

ABOUT THE AUTHOR

SAENA TELOW IS 16 YEARS OLD, and has been home educated all her life. *Dead Man's Coin* is her first novel.

Saena shares her writing on multiple social media platforms. On Wattpad, her work has been #1 in multiple hashtags. On TikTok, she maintains an interactive platform that inspires creativity in young people, and her writing there has received over a million views.